FORGOTTEN BY THE BILLIONAIRE

IT'S COMPLICATED - BOOK TWO

MAGGIE COLE

PULSE PRESS INC

PROLOGUE

Dr. Xander Kane

REALITY ISN'T ALWAYS WHAT WE PERCEIVE IT TO BE. WHAT'S REAL? What's fake? Is our truth of yesterday the truth of today?

I've been told I'm living in a fantasy, trying to regurgitate the past instead of moving into my future, but all I know as my truth is what my mind is telling me my heart should feel and what it should want.

I don't remember anyone except Billie. Well, except for the flash-backs. Night after night, I go to sleep, and I experience all of her except her face. She is a stranger.

Guilt crashes through me, as I should only be dreaming of Billie. She is the one I remember, not this faceless stranger. She is the one I love.

Or is she?

My friends tell me I don't love Billie. That we ended things long ago and weren't meant to be together. But how do I know that when it's all I remember?

How are my friends telling me the truth when all I feel is madly in love with Billie?

I search everywhere for her, but I can't find her. I spend my days searching social media, googling her name, walking streets in New York we used to stroll together. But she's nowhere.

The guys tell me I broke it off with Billie, and we were both better off because of it. But no one can tell me why I broke it off. No one can give me details. So, until I can find her, my heart belongs to her. It aches for her because all I remember is our love.

All day long, I'm obsessed. When my head hits the pillow, I dream. But it's never about Billie.

I hear the moan of a woman's voice against the curve of my neck. "Xander." A sound so unforgettable, I push it to the back of my mind throughout the day, as guilt shoots through me, and I try to refocus on my love for Billie.

I smell her scent—flowers after it rained.

I feel her gripping my back and trembling against me as our bodies sweat.

I see the perfect fit of her body wrapped against mine, clutching me.

I taste the salt of her skin and the sweetness of her tongue.

Blonde hair, the curve of her neck, the softness of her breasts, the plumpness of her red lips...it all flashes in my mind, torturing me.

She's so real in my dreams. Every night I go to sleep, I experience her. Everything I could ever know about her, except for her face and her name.

Daily, I tell myself it's just a dream. It's my brain playing games with me because it's still screwed up from the accident.

She isn't real.

She doesn't exist.

Or does she?

The thought sends my stomach flipping because that means I wasn't loyal to Billie. No matter what my friends tell me, I know what I had with Billie. I don't understand how it could have ended.

No. Surely they are wrong. It's a misunderstanding, and once I find Billie, whatever misunderstanding we had, we will work out.

Obsession takes hold of me. I can't move on until I find Billie. But she's nowhere.

Over the months, my memory slowly returns, except regarding Billie. I have no memories of dating or thinking about anyone except her. Everything else is clear—my medical school, my job, how to be a surgeon. But I have no memories of anyone in my life besides Billie.

But Billie didn't have blonde hair. She didn't smell like flowers after the rain or call out my name like the woman in my dreams.

I can't make sense of it all. If I can just find Billie, I can fix whatever went wrong between us. Then, this other woman will leave my dreams.

Or will she?

My phone rings, pushing my thoughts out of my head. "Hello, this is Xander."

"Xander, it's Angela Sincroy."

I sit up straighter. "Hi, Angela. How are you?"

"I'm good. You feeling better?"

"Yes."

"Great. We got the report from your doctor that you are fine to resume your normal surgical duties. We will need you to report to the hospital by Monday, or we will need to find another surgeon for the position."

"I'll be there."

"Great. See you next week." I hang up.

Life needs to resume. I can't stay home any longer and need to get back into a routine. My new role as a surgeon in Chicago is what I've worked hard for, and I'm not going to screw up my future.

Wandering over to the window, I glance out into the New York skyline. I'll pack up and move my life, but I won't stop the search. Until I find Billie, my heart won't be complete.

Charlotte

Present Day

"Welcome back," Jesse says when I step into the hospital.

"Thank you. It's great to be back." I smile at her and hold my leg in the air, flexing my foot and enjoying the freedom of not having any cast on it. My foot has fully healed, and I can resume all normal duties of my job.

"How long has it been?"

"Six months. I'm running behind, so I'll talk to you later, Jesse." I wave as I pass by her.

"Good to have you back, Charlotte."

I nod.

I'm not running behind. It's been a tough six months, and I don't want to discuss it. I want to forget about it and move on with my life.

After the car accident I was in with Xander, my entire life shifted.

Xander.

My heart still aches when I think of him. No matter how much I've tried to forget about him, I can't.

And I need to.

We only were together a few times. It shouldn't be a big deal. He doesn't remember me.

But it hurts.

Xander and I had a fire I had never experienced before. But it wasn't just the sex. He's funny, smart, and sexy. And we connected.

But he doesn't remember you, and you need to get over him, I remind myself for the millionth time.

I only visited him once after the accident. He had woken up from his medically induced coma. My friends didn't even tell me he was awake for several days, until I got discharged from the hospital.

"I need to tell you something," Piper gently said.

My gut dropped. It's like I knew bad news was coming. "What's that?"

Piper took a deep breath and shifted nervously on her feet. "It's about Xander."

My pulse increased. "Is he okay?"

Piper nodded. "Yes. He isn't in any danger."

"Okay..."

"He's been awake for several days."

My head almost snapped off my neck. "Why have you been lying to me?"

Piper took a deep breath. "He doesn't remember the last twelve years."

I tilted my head at her, confused. "What do you mean, he remembers nothing?"

She shook her head. "He thinks he's twenty-two and still dating his ex-girlfriend Billie."

No, he will remember me when he sees me.

I was wrong. Dead wrong.

When I went into Xander's room, he stared at me like a stranger. He gave me a polite smile and said, "I'm sorry, but I just don't remember you."

Piper, Quinn, and Vivian all insisted it probably was the medicine they still had him on and I should try again. But I knew better. I saw it in his eyes. He didn't remember me. And each time they suggested I try again, I asked if he still thought he was in love with Billie. They couldn't deny it, so I stayed away.

For the next several months, I recovered at Piper and Noah's place in New York. At first, they would ask me if I wanted to visit Xander with them, but I refused. I told Piper to stop updating me or mentioning his name. It was just too painful.

Unfortunately, I kept hearing their hushed conversations about how he was obsessed with finding his ex-girlfriend, Billie. How he kept telling Noah he loved her and wouldn't rest until he found her.

So, I've never seen him again. As soon as I could take care of myself, I moved back to Chicago.

My cast made it impossible for me to do all the duties of my job. I had to stay off my foot, which didn't allow me to be in the surgeries with the doctors and advise them on which medical devices they need to use for the operations.

Today is a new day, I tell myself, smiling as I walk down the hall and get into the elevator.

I love what I do, and I'm happy to be back. In the last few months, I've had too much time to sit and obsess over Xander and what could have been. I'm ready to immerse myself in my job and forget about whatever I thought we had.

The elevator stops, and I step off. I go into the locker room so I can get my scrubs on and prepare for my first surgery of the day. I open the door and run into my ex-boyfriend, Damon, who is also a medical device representative.

"Charlotte." He shifts on his feet and stands straighter. "How are you feeling?"

I smile. "Good. Fully recovered. Ready to get back to normal life."

He nods. "Well, looks like you'll have a full day. The schedule is packed."

"Sounds good to me. I've been bored out of my mind these last six months."

Damon's face hardens. "Yes, I remember you telling me."

My face heats as I think of the last time I saw him. I wish for the millionth time I could erase that memory from my bank.

"Have a good first day back, Charlotte."

I nod at him. "Thanks."

He leaves, and I sigh. Damon and I were hot and heavy for a while, but we lost our heat and never got it back. I broke up with him the week before I met Xander, and we haven't had the best history since I broke up with him. Then there was that one horrible night...

That wasn't too bad. Could have been a lot worse.

I open my locker and throw my belongings in it. I get ready for my surgery, knot my hair into a bun, and add my cap over it. The schedule is on the wall, and I locate the room of my first surgery.

When I arrive in the operating room, there's a team of people. I scrub my hands then move to the area where the nurse is putting gloves on anyone who will be participating in the surgery.

"Charlotte, you're back." Tabi grins at me.

"Yep. You're stuck with me now," I tease.

"Thank goodness. I've been in too many surgeries with Damon."

"What's wrong with Damon? He's good at what he does."

"He's been such a grouch since you dumped him."

I tilt my head and smirk at her. "Tabi, that was nine months ago. Surely he isn't still grouchy over that?"

"Girl, he's not been the same guy since you dumped him. I'm telling you—"

"Tabi, I think you've got better things to do than gossip?"

I turn.

"Charlotte! Good to have you back." Dr. Sear's eyes light up.

"Hey, Dr. Sear. How have you been?"

He nods. "Great. How's your foot?"

I lift my leg and flex my foot again. "All better. Ready to stand on it all day and watch you cut some people open."

He laughs. "I'm glad you're back. It's not been the same without you around here."

I smile. "I'm glad I'm back, too. It's been hard being away."

"I bet."

"So, who are we working with today?" I ask.

Dr. Sear points to a group of doctors already in their scrubs and standing around the patient who is being administered an IV of anesthesia. "The typical crew, except for one new surgeon who has come on board since you left. Come on over, and I'll introduce you."

Tabi puts surgical masks over my face and Dr. Sear's. We walk over to the huddle of doctors.

"DeVoe! You're back." Dr. Wemer grins at me.

I give him a little salute. "In the flesh," I joke.

"Glad to have you back."

"Thought you left us for good. Nice to see you're back." Dr. Pinner gives me a fist bump in the air without touching my fist. "Glad to know you aren't leaving us with Damon for the rest of our lives."

I laugh. Apparently, Damon hasn't made any friends.

"How did you date that guy for so long?" Dr. Wemer asks.

I roll my eyes and don't answer his question. "It couldn't have been that bad."

"Don't sell yourself short. You've been missed," Dr. Pinner says.

I laugh. "Glad you didn't forget about me during my recovery."

"Charlotte! Rock, paper, scissors! One, two, three." Dr. Croy holds his hand out in paper while I make scissors. "Damn it! I always lose!"

I throw my arm in the air in a victory pump. "Club Hip Hop Radio. All day."

He groans.

I turn to meet the new doctor and my heart about stops in my chest. My smile falls. A surgical mask covers his face, but I know those eyes. They've haunted me over the last six months.

I seriously must have messed up in my past life. Whoever is in charge of karma hates me.

Dr. Sear says, "Charlotte, meet our newest surgeon, Dr. Xander Kane."

"Dr. Kane, meet Charlotte DeVoe. She was in a bad car accident and her foot was reconstructed. She was out of work for the last six months, but it's our lucky day because she's back. Charlotte's the best rep we have." Dr. Sear beams at me then Xander.

Xander stares at me, and I stare back at him.

He's only staring at you because this is uncomfortable and he doesn't know what to say.

What do you expect him to say? She's the girl I screwed several nights and got into the car accident with? Oh, but I don't remember her and am obsessed over my ex-girlfriend who I haven't been with in a decade?

Does he even know it's me?

I recover quickly and nod at him. "It's nice to meet you."

He blinks then nods. "I'm glad to hear your foot is okay."

"Thanks. Welcome to the hospital." I turn to Dr. Croy so I don't have to look at Xander. "Isn't my music supposed to be on?"

Maybe my music will tune out my thoughts about Xander so I can get through this.

Dr. Croy groans and turns the channel on.

The anesthesiologist announces, "You're good to start."

I let out a breath. *Just concentrate on the surgery and forget he's here.*

But I can't. My pulse is beating against my throat and I want to run out of the room. I try to ignore him, but it's impossible.

From time to time, we catch the other person staring. I wonder if he knows it is me or if he just thinks I'm some other girl named Charlotte who broke her foot.

The surgery is long. We are reconstructing several bones in the patient's leg, and there has been excessive damage. It is scheduled to take four hours but ends up taking seven.

As luck has it, I spend almost the entire surgery next to Xander, as Dr. Sear instructs him to do a lot of the work I'm needed to advise on.

When I first approach, he freezes. It's not something the other doctors would have noticed, but I do.

Does he know it's me?

As quickly as his paralysis comes, it goes, and he soon is back into his routine of surgery.

Not only do I have to remain near him but talk to him and hand him different devices. And it's clear to me he's brilliant at what he does. He's miles ahead of many surgeons I've worked with and another reminder he's amazing but I can't have him.

I spend seven hours with my heart beating way too fast, feeling the electrical buzz of him next to me, and trying to not get excited every time my name rolls off his tongue.

For six months I attempted to forget about his voice. It's like a cruel joke the universe is playing on me, and I do my best to maintain my professionalism.

And every single time I see his bright brown eyes, my soul is crushed further.

As soon as the surgery is over, I leave the operating room and head to the locker room.

I need to get out of here.

I don't realize it until I reach to unlock my locker, but I'm shaking. I'm having a hard time with the combination when I hear, "Charlotte."

Closing my eyes, I breathe a few times, grab my hair cap, and pull it off. I don't know why I pull it off right then, but I do.

I turn to Xander, blinking back the tears I wish weren't there.

Xander

SHE SEEMS FAMILIAR. SOMETHING ABOUT HER SEEMS FAMILIAR.

I'm watching her interact with the other surgeons when Dr. Croy says her name.

Charlotte.

But it can't be. I know Piper and her friends are from Chicago, but surely it's not her?

When I woke in the hospital, Noah told me Billie wasn't in the accident with me. He said a girl named Charlotte, who was Piper's friend, was in the car and that we had spent the night together a few times.

She came to see me in the hospital after I had been awake a few days, but I was on a lot of medication, and it was foggy.

The encounter is still a blur because I don't remember much about it. And I don't remember the face of the woman named Charlotte who came to see me.

I can't see this woman's face, but the way she tries to avoid looking at me gives me the impression she knows me. My gut is telling me I've hurt her.

Throughout the surgery, I instruct myself to stay focused, not to try to figure out who she is or what our relationship could have been. Besides, I could be misjudging everything.

At one point, I could trust my brain, but since the accident, so much of my life is unclear, I don't have the same faith in it I used to.

But then she stands right near me, and I know our pasts are somehow connected. She smells like flowers after the rain.

As soon as the surgery is through, she excuses herself and bolts out of the operating room. I try not to run after her so I don't cause a scene.

I scan the locker room when I walk through the door. No one is there except Charlotte. She's trying to get her locker open, and her hand is shaking.

"Charlotte," I say, and she pauses then rips off her surgical cap, revealing her blonde hair. My heart stops.

She turns, gripping her cap tight and blinking back tears in her blue eyes. Her plump red lips are slightly shaking. My heart swells, and I don't understand it, because I don't remember her, but I know it's her. It's the woman who's been haunting my dreams.

A strange combination of guilt and excitement fills me, and I'm paralyzed for a moment. She isn't Billie. She is another woman.

But I have all these emotions toward her I shouldn't be feeling for anyone besides Billie. And they are flying at me hard.

She's beyond gorgeous. Everything about her is perfect. But I've hurt her. It's clear to me I have, but I don't know what I've done.

She turns away from me, staring at her locker, and wipes a tear off her cheek.

My heart feels like it's ripping out of my chest.

"Charlotte?"

She puts her hand on her locker, as if to steady herself, then faces me. "Xander."

Xander. The only word she ever says in my dream. It's her. There is no doubt about it. No matter how mushed up my brain might be, I'd know that voice saying my name anywhere. It lives in my head all day long.

"I've hurt you." I say it as a statement and not a question.

She bites her bottom lip and says nothing, continuing to blink back tears.

A wave of regret rolls through me, and my eyes fill, too. "I'm sorry. I don't know what I've done. Can you tell me?"

The dam breaks, tears rush down both of her cheeks, and she shakes her head in small little movements.

She's like a magnet, and I step forward, not thinking, not even considering Billie, and cup her face in my hands, wiping her cheeks with my thumbs. "I dream of you," I whisper, not thinking before I speak.

Her eyes widen and more droplets fall. "You remember me?"

I shake my head. "Not outside my dreams."

She's silent.

"Can you tell me what I've done?" I repeat.

"Are you still searching for Billie?"

"Yes," I say, without even thinking.

"Because you love her?"

"Yes."

She moves my hands off her face and takes a deep breath. "You have done nothing intentional to hurt me."

"No?"

"No." She turns and unlocks her locker.

"Charlotte—"

"Everything is fine, Xander. I hope you find Billie and are happy." She opens her locker, slings her bag over her shoulder, and shuts the door.

"Charlotte—"

She puts a finger over my mouth. "It's okay. We have to work together. Let's not talk about this again."

I stand stunned, not sure what I've done but knowing I've done something, as she leaves the locker room.

————

My shift ends around two in the afternoon. Surgery started early in the morning, and as soon as I'm done I go back to the hotel I'm staying and call Noah.

He answers the phone. "Xander, how was your first day?"

"I need to talk to you."

"You okay?"

"Yeah. All's good. You around later?"

"Sure. You want to go grab a beer?"

"Sounds good. Just text me an address. I don't know where anything in this city is."

Noah laughs. "I know the feeling, Don't worry though. It's smaller than New York, and you'll learn it quickly."

"All right. I'll go work out. Meet around five?"

"Sure. I'll send the address."

"Thanks."

"You sure you're okay?" Noah asks.

"Yeah. Don't worry. I'll meet you at the bar." I disconnect.

After throwing on a pair of sneakers, I quickly leave my hotel room and find the running path. I don't know my way around the city, but I stay on the track, twisting through the city and around the lake. When I'm about six miles out, I turn around and follow the same route back.

The entire run, I'm sorting through confusing thoughts in my head.

Why can't I find Billie?

What was my relationship with Charlotte? I know we've had sex. We had to have, based on my dreams. Plus, Noah told me I stayed with her a few nights. But what happened those nights?

Why did I feel all those emotions when I saw her?

What about Billie?

I'm not closer to any answers after my run than before, and I'm even more frustrated.

When I get done running, I'm drenched in sweat, and my heart is beating hard. I put my hands on the back of my head and jog another mile to cool down, trying to get the faces of both Billie and Charlotte out of my mind.

But it's impossible.

I finally head back into the hotel, go up to my room, and shower. Noah sends me the address. It's a bar, not too far away from the hotel. I've got time, so I use the map on my phone and walk.

I've lived in New York City my entire life and love everything about it. Chicago is a big city but not as big as New York. While everyone is hustling about, just like New York, it still feels different.

Noah moved within the last year, and I know he struggled a bit, transitioning. I suspect it will be easier for me since he's here.

When I get to the bar, Noah fist-bumps me, and I sit down, just as the waitress comes over with two beers on a tray.

She tries to flirt with Noah and me, but we don't engage. When she leaves, Noah leans into the table. "What's going on? You sure you are okay?"

Noah has been my friend almost my entire life. We've been through everything together. He knows me better than anyone. Hell, he may know me better than I know myself right now, based on my memory issues.

I sigh. "Tell me about Charlotte."

He jerks his head at me. "You remember her?"

While I tap my fingers on the table, my pulse feels like it's going to beat through my neck. I've never disclosed to anyone, including Noah, that I have dreams every night about a woman that isn't Billie.

"I just went through a seven-hour surgery with her."

Noah's eyes widen. "Wow. What happened?"

"I've hurt her."

"Xander, what happened? Tell me."

I take a big gulp of beer, not tasting it. "I'll tell you everything, but I want you to explain what happened with Billie and me. I know you're holding something back from me."

Noah shakes his head. "I've told you everything there is to know. Anything you've ever told me. Why would I hide something from you?"

Sitting back farther in the booth, I sigh. "It doesn't make sense to me. We just broke up?"

"Yes. You were working as a paramedic and putting yourself through medical school. Billie didn't like your schedule. In fairness, she hardly saw you. You really had a crazy schedule."

"So, she left me?"

"No. She gave you an ultimatum. Her parents said they would pay for your medical school so you could quit your paramedic job, but you wouldn't do that."

I jerk my head back. "I wouldn't. She would know that."

Noah nods. "Yes. You broke it off with her, but it was mutual. You wanted different things."

"But we loved each other."

"You were in your twenties and grew apart. Both of you were trying to hold onto something that wasn't working anymore. It happens."

I cover my face with my hands for a moment, trying to wrap my brain around this and hoping to remember anything Noah has told me, but I can't. Nothing comes to mind.

"I just wish I could remember."

Noah sighs. "It will eventually come to you. The doctors are convinced. Maybe don't try so hard."

"This is so frustrating. All I can remember is Billie was who I wanted to spend the rest of my life with. We talked about getting married once I graduated. How does that change?"

"Xander, you grew apart. It happens. You need to come to terms with it and stop this search you have going on."

I stare at him. "I can't. Until I remember or find her and talk to her, I just can't. You don't understand what this is like for me."

"Okay, man. Tell me what happened with Charlotte."

My heart races, and I swallow hard. I don't know why I'm nervous to tell him this, but I feel like I'm somehow cheating on Billie. The reality is I'm not, based on what Noah is telling me about our relationship, but guilt consumes me.

"Xander, whatever it is, tell me."

"I dream of her."

"Of Billie?"

I clear my throat. "Charlotte."

Noah's eyes widen. "You remember her? That's great!"

I shake my head. "No. You don't understand. I dream of her. I smell her. Feel her. Taste her. Experience everything about her but never see her face. I hear her say my name."

Noah stays quiet.

I rub my hands on my face then take another tasteless sip of beer.

"What happened today?"

"I was in surgery, and they introduced me to her. She had her surgical mask on and cap covering her hair. Her eyes looked so familiar. Then they informed me about her accident and foot, so it seemed too coincidental for her not to be the same Charlotte you told me was in the car with me." I pause and take another deep breath. "Then I smelled her. I knew it was her...the woman in my dreams."

Noah continues to stare at me. I'm not sure what is going through his mind. He finally says, "Go on."

"After the surgery, she left as soon as possible, and I waited long enough so it wouldn't seem like I was following her. I went into the locker room and...and..." I put my hands over my face. Charlotte's eyes full of tears plague my mind, and my heart splinters once more.

A few minutes pass. I have to regain my composure. I blink hard when I think of her pained expression.

I gaze up at Noah. "She wouldn't tell me what I did to hurt her. But I know I have. I saw it. She was crying, and I caused it. She asked me if I was still searching for Billie, and I responded yes, then she asked if I still loved Billie, and I said yes. Charlotte told me to keep it professional and never talk about this to her again."

"Shit," Noah mutters.

"Noah, what did I do?"

He takes a deep breath. "Piper thinks you broke Charlotte's heart."

"How?"

"After the accident, she cried for days about seeing you. We kept telling her she couldn't because you were in a coma. When Piper finally told her you were awake and didn't remember the last twelve years, and about Billie, she thought when you saw her, you would recognize her. She came to see you in the hospital, and you had no memory of her."

"I don't even remember that. I was on so much medication. What did I say to her?"

"You politely said, 'I'm sorry, but I just don't remember you,' then you turned away and asked me about Billie."

My gut drops. "Crap. I'm an asshole."

Noah shakes his head. "You were on a lot of drugs still. We tried to get her to visit you again, but she kept asking if you were still searching for Billie. We didn't want to lie to her. It's why I asked you to go see her when you were still in New York."

"You said we were only together a few times?"

Noah nods.

"I don't understand why she's so heartbroken, then. Or why I keep dreaming about her."

Noah laughs. "Let's just say after the first night you were together, you were praying she didn't get a boyfriend before you moved here."

"How did we meet?"

"You came to visit me. We were at Club D, and I saw Piper. Charlotte, Quinn, and Vivian were with Piper. You had just accepted the job in Chicago."

"And that's the first night I slept with her?"

Noah nods.

"Why was she in New York?"

"I was there for the First Responders Charity Date Auction with Piper. We were all in the back getting changed, and Piper texted the girls and Charlotte bid on you."

"She bid on me?"

Noah smiles. "Yep. She paid over three grand for you."

I gape at him. "Seriously?"

He laughs. "Yep. And she flew out to New York to surprise you for your date the night before you got into the crash."

"But we've only seen each other a few times?"

Noah nods. "I think you were texting and talking a lot though."

"I don't understand this. If we only saw each other a few times..." I tilt my head in confusion. How can I feel what I felt when I saw her today?

Noah chuckles. "You're trying to rationalize the heart, Xander. You can't do that. The heart wants what the heart wants. I think whatever happened between you and Charlotte was intense."

"But, I still love Billie." It's not making sense to me.

"You don't love Billie," Noah sternly says to me for the hundredth time over the last six months.

"I hear what you say, Noah, but my mind tells me otherwise."

"You really remember nothing about the years between twenty-two and twenty-four when you and Billie were together?"

I shake my head.

"If you could remember those years, you would understand. You two fought all the time. Neither of you were happy, and you started to see less and less of each other."

I rub my forehead hard and stare at Noah, beyond frustrated. "I just can't remember any of it."

Noah sighs. "Besides your dreams, do you remember anything about your time with Charlotte?"

I wrack my brain again. "No. And I'm not sure how to get my memories back."

Charlotte

Nine Months Earlier

THE LADIES AND I ARE AT CLUB D WHEN PIPER TELLS US SHE'S screwing her new boss, Noah. She's claiming he's an asshole, and it won't be happening again, when Noah appears behind her with the most attractive man I've ever laid eyes on.

He's tall, muscular but not over-the-top, and has dark-brown hair and beautiful brown eyes. Our gazes meet briefly before he turns back to Noah.

"What are you doing here?" Piper hurls at Noah.

"This is my friend Xander. He's moving to Chicago and in town for the weekend. We're out...like you," Noah teases her.

"Ha ha." Piper rolls her eyes and shoots Noah daggers.

"Piper, who are your friends?" I ask.

"This is my boss, Noah, and his friend Xander." Piper nods at Xander, who gives her a friendly smile. Xander grins at all of us girls, and maybe it's wishful thinking, but I swear his focus lingers longest on me.

"Oh, your boss," Vivian says, and us girls all giggle. Piper's face gets beet red before she glares at us to behave.

"Do you guys want to join us?" Quinn asks, moving over to make room.

"Don't mind if we do." Noah sits down as close to Piper as he can get.

Xander sits down next to Quinn and shakes her hand then Vivian's. "Charlotte, nice to meet you." He takes my hand, and strokes the back with his thumb.

Wait. Did that happen, or am I imagining it?

His brown eyes have a golden twinkle, and his mouth curves upward.

I smile back, and my face heats

When he lets go, Vivian asks, "So you're moving here, Xander?"

"In a few months. I just accepted a surgeon's position at the hospital."

My heart beats faster. He will be living here, and he's a doctor?

"You're a surgeon?" I ask him.

Pride crosses his face. "Yes."

"What kind?"

"Orthopedic."

"That sounds exciting," Quinn says.

Xander laughs. "It would probably gross all of you out."

"Do you like the blood or the pus more?" I throw out there.

His head jerks toward me, and a surprised grin forms on his face. "Are you into blood and pus?"

"Okay, you two are gross." Vivian wrinkles her nose.

"I'm a fan of the pus more than the blood. The blood is predictable. The pus isn't."

"You just crossed the disgusting line, Charlotte," Quinn mutters.

Xander's face lights up. "Are you a doctor?"

I laugh. "No, I'm an orthopedic medical device rep, and I'm in a lot of surgeries, assisting the doctors.

"Really?" he asks.

I nod.

"So, you dig surgery and all its gore?"

I laugh. "Can't get enough of it."

Xander licks his lips. "That's pretty hot."

My face heats up.

Quinn clears her throat. "Excuse me. I need to go to the ladies' room."

"I'll go with you," Vivian says.

Xander stands up but doesn't take his eyes off me. Quinn and Vivian leave, and I realize Noah and Piper are on the dance floor. Xander sits down right next to me. The deliciously clean, raw smell of his skin makes my pulse throb.

"Before I go any further and make an ass of myself, are you single?" Xander asks.

I flush deeper. "As of last week, yes."

His eyes don't leave mine. "Who broke up with whom?"

"I broke up with him."

"Why?"

"There wasn't any heat." It comes out of my mouth without even thinking, and my face is scorching.

Xander licks his lips again. "You want to dance?"

I smirk at him. "I don't know. Do you know how to dance?"

He laughs and stands up, clasps my hand, and rubs his thumb on it again. "There's only one way for you to find out." He pulls me up, right against him. I gaze up at his face. "By the way, you're gorgeous."

I'm not sure how many shades of red my face can burn, but I'm pretty sure it's full-on maroon.

He strokes my cheek. "Let's go." He leads me out to the crowded dance floor, and we quickly fall into a perfect rhythm based on whatever song the DJ plays.

Several songs in, a random guy tries to cut in, but Xander pulls me so close to him, I can feel his heartbeat. He leans down and brings his mouth to my ear. "I'm claiming you as mine tonight unless you have any objections?"

An excited flutter rolls through me. Nope, no objections. *I will be yours*, I think.

Xander presses his forehead to mine, waiting for me to answer him, staring at me intensely with his beautiful, brown eyes. I lace my fingers around the back of his head. "No objections."

He smiles then brushes his lips against mine. His tongue parts my lips, gently at first, then with more urgency and passion, stoking a fire so hot, I'm left breathless and craving more.

No one around us exists. It's just Xander and me, staring, smiling, and grinding against each other.

My body is humming against his. He wraps his hands and arms around me, holding me tight and claiming me.

"Drink?" he shouts in my ear, and I nod. He clasps my hand and puts his other palm on the small of my back, guiding me to the bar. "What do you want to drink, Charlotte?"

"Water," I tell him.

He orders two bottles and leads me back to our table. Quinn and Vivian give me a knowing glance as Xander sits down and pulls me onto his lap.

He's about to say something when his phone vibrates. He looks at his phone then at me. "Is Piper's purse here?"

I point to her purse.

Xander types something.

"What's going on?" Quinn asks.

"Noah and Piper left. She forgot her purse. Can one of you take it and give it to her tomorrow?"

Vivian grabs it. "I'll take it."

"So Piper is going to Noah's?"

Xander nods.

"Is that where you are staying?" I say so only he can hear.

His thumb makes a circular motion on my thigh. "That was the plan, but it's changeable."

I stare in his eyes. "Is that your way of saying you want to stay at my place?"

He grins. "If you ask, I'll say yes. If you don't ask, I won't take offense."

I've never had a one-night stand before, but something about Xander makes me feel like it's okay. I lean into his ear. "I don't invite strangers to my house, but I'm going to make an exception for you."

He pecks me on the lips then texts something, I presume to Noah. "That's done. Are you ready to go, or do you want to stay and dance more?"

Butterflies take off in my stomach.

He must sense my nerves. "We won't do anything you don't want to," he assures me.

"I'm ready to go if you are."

He stands up and tells Quinn and Vivian it's been nice meeting them.

They both smirk at me, and I give them a quick wave before Xander guides me through the crowded club. When we get outside, we quickly jump in a cab. I give the cabbie my address.

"Do you live alone or have roommates?" Xander asks.

"Alone."

"Good." He kisses my jawline.

"Good?"

"Mm-hmm," he murmurs.

"Mm-hmm?"

"We don't have to worry about being quiet." His lips on the curve of my neck send little flutters through my body.

"You plan on being loud?" I tease.

"I plan on you being loud," he whispers then gently sucks on my earlobe and strokes the inside of my thigh, as shivers run down my spine.

I inhale deeply, close my eyes, then moan softly as his lips trace my jawline again and finally meet my mouth. His delicious tongue swirls around mine, arousing waves of desire and a need I haven't experienced before.

Xander positions me on his lap and kisses me as no man has ever done before. In his arms, against his body, I melt into him, wanting everything he can give me.

The driver stops in front of my building, and Xander throws some cash at him. He quickly leads me into the lobby and to the elevator. Before the doors shut, he picks me up and pushes me against the wall, and I wrap my legs around him before I even think about it.

"How the hell are you single," he mutters.

I want to ask him the same thing, but that would require a conversation and me to stop kissing him, and I don't want to take my lips away from his.

My body has never reacted to anyone's like this before. The dress I'm wearing is scrunched up, and I'm grinding my wet heat against his hard erection.

The elevator doors open, and we're still in the lobby. "Charlotte, what floor is your place on?" he mumbles.

I laugh. "Fifteen."

Xander quickly scans the panel and pushes the button then returns his lips to mine.

I circle my lower body on him, repeatedly, and his deep, throaty groan ricochets in the air.

I'M SO WET, I WONDER IF I'M RUINING HIS PANTS.

"Oh, you turn me on," he breathes into me as I push my lower body against him harder, panting for air, desperate for him to make me soar.

The elevator opens and he grabs around my waist, steps out of it, and growls, "What's your apartment number?"

"Fifteen twenty-eight," I barely get out and wrap my arms tight around his shoulders before I push my lips back to his.

At my door, he sets me down so I can get out my key, but he presses his body to the back of mine. His mouth is on my neck, and his hand lightly grazes my dress, right on top of my sex.

When I finally get my key out, my hand is shaking, and he laughs softly before helping me unlock the door.

It's dark inside, and I don't bother to turn on the light, I just take his hand and pull him into the bedroom.

I'm hot and sticky from the club. Normally, it takes me a while dating someone before I'm comfortable enough to stand naked with them and shower, but I don't feel the slightest bit uncomfortable with Xander.

"Do you want to shower with me?" I ask him. It's dark besides what filters in from the streetlights, but I've adjusted and his bright orbs light up.

He brushes his fingers on my cheek. "Is that really a question?"

I exhale slowly and he reaches around to the back of my dress, moves my hair aside and tugs the zipper down, pushing the dress to the floor. He stands back and whistles, checking me out in my hot-pink, barely there thong and push-up bra.

My cheeks flame.

"You really have no clue, do you?"

"About?" I tilt my head in question.

"How unbelievably gorgeous you are." His eyes drill into mine, as if he can see the depths of my soul, and a million butterflies take off in my stomach.

I step forward and remove his shirt then release his belt. I realize he's letting me undress him, a smile curling the edges of his lips as my shaky hands liberate his cock from his pants.

His body shines in the dimness, beautiful and glowing, with pre-cum already on the tip of his erection.

My fingers graze his shaft then I palm it and circle the cap with my thumb, as my lips flutter against his chest.

Xander groans, and the intensity in his eyes turns my insides into Jell-O. He reaches around, releases my bra from my body, and slides my panties to the floor. "God, I want to taste you."

Adrenaline spurts through my body at the thought, but I clasp his hand. "Shower. I need a shower."

He gives me a cocky glance, lets me lead him to the shower, then reaches in and turns on the water. The water quickly heats up and we step in. He picks up my bottle of body wash, pours it in his hand and massages it into me, kneading his fingers all over and rubbing his body against mine.

As the soap rinses away, he bends down to kiss me. I wrap my arms around his shoulders and he pushes me against the wall, kneels down, and kisses my breasts then my stomach, before picking me up and throwing my legs over his shoulders.

"Oh God," I cry out, quivering as he unleashes the divinity of his tongue upon my pussy.

Exploring me.

Entering me.

Exciting me.

He groans against my clit as I whimper. His warm hands on my hips, I buck into his face, soaring higher and higher, close to the edge of euphoria.

Steam is all around us, eliciting tiny beads of sweat.

The heat of his tongue glides in a pattern of flicks and sucks, increasing his speed and pressure.

I throb. My arms and torso fall forward, and I grip his head, holding him in place. "Xander...oh...don't stop...oh...God!"

At a harder flick of his tongue, I erupt against his face, trembling against the wall, grasping my hands against his head hard, calling out his name.

I'm still quivering inside and, when my high is over, he gently sets me back on the floor. Moving his way up, he rolls his tongue over my areolas. A new heat flares throughout my lower region.

And I want him in me. More than any man I've ever been with, I want Xander inside me. Before I know what's coming out of my mouth, I breathlessly blurt out something I've never said to any man before. "I want you."

He presses his forehead to mine, staring at me with eyes that scream adoration and desire. "Let's get out of here."

I nod and he turns off the water, reaches out of the shower, and picks up a towel. He dries every drop of water off of me, kissing my shoulder, neck, and lips, keeping my loins on fire for him.

Xander quickly dries himself off then leads me to my bedroom.

Reaching in my drawer, I grab a strip of condoms. I push him on the bed and crawl on top of him, straddling him, tear the condom open, and roll it over his hard shaft.

He caresses the back of my head and he pulls me into his mouth while his other hand squeezes my hip.

I whimper in his mouth and he groans into mine as his cock sinks into my wet sex, filling me, making me whole.

Rocking my hips, I take more of him in me.

Slipping around him.

Savoring every inch he will give me.

Spasming against his throbbing heat.

"Oh, you're heaven," he whispers in my ear then nibbles and sucks on my lobe.

Blood hums, pulsing with adrenaline, vibrating all my cells, as the warmth and touch of Xander creates a level of heat I've never felt before.

"Xander," I moan into the curve of his neck.

His arms blanket me, pulling me tight, and creating a sense of safety I'm not used to.

The warmth of his tongue glides over my collarbone as our bodies sweat and slide together.

I grip him, digging into his back, clutching his hardness, ready to come unhinged in his arms.

"Oh..." I breathe out as dizziness encroaches upon me.

"You're so good," Xander mumbles then holds my head and creates a new feeling of euphoria in my mouth, sending jolts of energy throughout all my cells.

He pushes his forehead to mine, and I tighten my arms around him, vibrating on his cock, whimpering.

"I...I... Oh..."

He pushes my hair off my face, and his other hand pushes my hip down on him harder.

"Oh fuck," I yell out in the most powerful orgasm I've ever had.

"Charlotte," he groans, pumping hard into me, sending me further into my climax.

When we come down, his intense eyes stare into mine, and a smile plays upon his lips.

He slides me off him and pushes me down to the bed so I'm lying on his arm. His body is propped on its side next to mine. "Tell me again how you're single?"

I laugh.

"I don't expect a girl like you to wait for me, but if you're still single when I move here, can I see you again?"

4

Charlotte

Present Day

As quickly as I can walk away from Xander, I do. My heart is beating harder, and I focus on the floor until I get out of the hospital, too scared to look at anyone, for fear I'm going to break down and sob hysterically.

He dreams of me.

But he is still searching for and loves Billie.

Stay away.

My brain is a mishmash of thoughts, with the most dangerous one of all springing to the surface, over and over again.

Hope.

I need to get it out of my system. There is no future with Xander. He will never let go of his feelings for this Billie woman, whoever she is.

When the doors to the hospital open and I step outside, I pick my head up. With the cold wind beating on my face, I scurry to the parking garage and locate my car. Only once I'm inside it do I break down.

Seven hours of torture. That's what I endured. Every second wondering if he knew who I was or didn't. But then he came into the locker room and gave me a glimmer of hope that he remembered me.

But he doesn't.

He told me he dreams of me, but what does that mean? How can he dream of me but not remember me?

Then he touched me. He held my face in his hands and through tear-filled eyes, wanted to know how he hurt me.

I almost told him.

I almost wrapped my arms around him and cried into his chest.

Almost.

There were so many emotions in his eyes: confusion, fear, frustration. I saw it all, and it ripped my heart into tinier pieces.

As much as I wanted to tell him, it wasn't fair, not to me, nor him. He was going through enough pain from losing his memory.

If I told him what he did, I inevitably would end up in his arms, and it would just be him trying to comfort me. I'd be wrecked further. If he knew why he hurt me, he'd feel more guilt. It wasn't his fault he couldn't remember or that he still loved Billie.

So I didn't tell him because it wasn't fair. I knew from my childhood, life wasn't fair and how hard it was.

Growing up in an orphanage with no one to love or care for me, fair was not something that ever entered my life. I tried not to let my past turn me into a victim, not to let it harden my heart. But for once, I wish the universe would give me just a bit of fairness.

But it just wasn't in the cards for me.

So, I spared Xander from it and took all the pain for myself. Out of all the things I've been through, this feels the worst, and I don't know how that's possible.

I only spent a few nights with him. Every day, for several months, we communicated every way possible, but logically, this pain I feel shouldn't be this deep.

It was only a few days.

Then again, we told each other our secrets. I shared things I hadn't shared with anyone I had dated before. And we declared our love and made promises to one other.

But I will take on more pain to shield Xander. He didn't deserve to lose his memory. It's my fault we were in the accident anyway. If I hadn't flown in to surprise him, he wouldn't have insisted on driving me to the airport. We wouldn't have gotten into the accident, and his memory wouldn't be gone.

If I hadn't allowed him to drive me, we would be together right now.

I can't imagine what he is going through, and even though I can't have him, I want him to be guilt-free and happy, even if it's with Billie.

I sit in my car sobbing so hard, it takes me a while to pull myself together enough to drive home.

When I get there, I curl up in a ball on my bed. I need to figure out a way to work next to him and not feel like this. Now that he's in Chicago and our paths have crossed professionally, I'm going to have to deal with it. I can't be breaking down every time I'm around him.

I'm trying to figure out a strategy of how to forget him when I hear my buzzer. I go over and hit the intercom.

"Let me in, Charlotte." Quinn's voice comes through the speaker.

Why is Quinn here? I wrack my brain then remember the girls and I planned to go out for dinner and drinks to celebrate my first day back. I hit the buzzer, and it doesn't take long till Quinn is standing in my apartment.

When she steps in, she gives me a big hug. "How was your first day back?"

I lie to her. "Fine."

She tilts her head and squints at me. "Charlotte, have you been crying?"

I turn away.

Quinn puts her arm around my shoulder. "Hey, what's wrong?"

My stomach shakes again. "I was in surgery all day with Xander."

"What? Come sit down." She pulls me over to the couch.

"He's in Chicago, the new surgeon on my team of doctors. For seven hours, I had to work next to him."

Quinn puts her hand over her mouth. Then she removes it and asks, "Does he remember you."

I scan Quinn's eyes, not sure if I should tell her.

"What? Tell me."

"He doesn't remember me but told me he dreams about me."

She arches a brow. "So, he remembers you."

I shake my head. "He is still searching for Billie and loves her."

"Xander doesn't love her. He doesn't remember everything but will realize it eventually."

I shake my head harder. "No. He's in love with her. I asked him, and he didn't even hesitate."

Quinn's eyes widen. "But if he dreams of you, then he remembers you. His mind must be trying to piece things together."

"No, he doesn't remember me. And I can't live in hope. I need to forget about him and move on. I won't stand in the way of him finding Billie or play second fiddle if he is still in love with another woman."

"But he isn't," Quinn insists. "Jamison says once his memory of when he was twenty-two to twenty-four comes back fully, he will realize he hasn't loved her in over ten years."

I need to change the subject, so I flip the tables on Quinn. "What's going on with you and Jamison?"

Her face flushes, and she shrugs. "Nothing. We're friends. Not much can go on when we live a plane ride away."

I narrow my eyes and stay silent.

"What?"

"I don't believe nothing is going on."

"That's your choice."

"But if you were in the same city, you would be together?"

She flushes darker and shrugs again.

I tilt my head. "I'll take that as a yes."

She avoids my observation. "What are you going to do about Xander?"

"I don't know. I'm going to have to work with him. I need to forget about him."

Quinn squints at me. "Why don't you see if you hang out with him if he remembers you?"

"No way. He's in love with another woman. There's—"

"But he isn't. He doesn't love her anymore. He just doesn't remember. Once he does, it won't be an issue. Jamison swears he was over her way before he met you."

"Whether he was over her before we met doesn't matter. What matters is right now, he is in love with her."

"But—"

"No!" I'm almost yelling.

Quinn slowly nods. "Okay."

I glance down at my watch. "We'd better get going, or we'll be late meeting the girls."

Quinn stands.

I rise, too. "I don't want to talk about this with the others. I shouldn't have said anything to you."

"Why?"

"Xander and I are over. It will never be. Let's just drop it, okay?"

Quinn sighs. "If that's what you want."

"It is." But it's the farthest thing from what I want.

————

QUINN AND I GET TO THE RESTAURANT, AND PIPER AND VIVIAN ARE already there. They have drinks waiting for us on the table, and as soon as I sit down, I chug half of mine back.

"Jeez, Charlotte. Thirsty?" Vivian teases.

"Yep." I motion for the waitress to send me another drink.

Quinn glances at me, and I know she is dying to spill my Xander news. I give her a look that tells her I'm going to kill her if she says a word.

I do not want to talk about it.

Unfortunately, like my luck has been all day, that isn't in the cards.

Piper clears her throat. "Since you've got a drink in you now, I need to tell you something."

I know what's coming. I don't know why I thought I would get away with avoiding the Xander topic tonight.

"Xander is moving here, and he started at the hospital you work at," Piper blurts out.

I sarcastically laugh. "Yeah, I figured that out after the seven-hour surgery I had to endure with him today."

"Seven hours!" Vivian shrieks.

I throw back the rest of my drink then glare at Piper. Suddenly, I'm mad. She could have prepared me for my run-in with Xander. "Thanks for having my back on that one."

Piper winces. "You said you didn't want to know anything about how he was doing. I wanted to tell you in person. I'm sorry. I didn't know."

"I don't think Xander working at the same hospital I do is in the same classification as status updates on him," I throw back at her.

"I'm sorry. You're right."

Vivian puts her hand on mine. "What happened?"

The waitress sets down another martini, and I take a sip. I tell the girls everything that happened, including how Xander said he dreams of me.

"What does that mean?" Vivian asks.

I shrug. "I don't know. He doesn't remember me, but he dreams of me. How does that even make sense?"

I don't get any answers, just confused stares. I can't say I blame my friends.

"What did he say you are doing in these dreams?" Quinn asks.

I shrug. "We didn't get that far. But it doesn't matter. He is still searching for and in love with Billie."

After finishing my second martini, I pop the green olive in my mouth and ask the waitress for water. I rarely drink a lot, and it's already going to my head.

I tap my fingers on the table and stare at Piper. "I assume Xander is staying with you and Noah?"

She shakes her head. "The hospital is paying for his accommodations until he finds a place. It's part of his relocation package, and he said he didn't want to be in our hair. We told him that was silly, but he chose to stay at the hotel."

It's on the tip of my tongue to ask her which one, but I don't. I'm afraid I might use my liquid courage and end up beating on his door tonight.

Quinn says, "I told Charlotte I think they just need to hang out, and he will remember her."

"No," I sternly tell her again.

"Why? It won't hurt," Vivian says.

I sarcastically laugh. "It won't hurt? Who? Xander? Because it will definitely hurt me, and I already hurt enough."

"You don't know that." Piper points at me.

"My heart is crushed enough. I don't need to set myself up to get trampled even more. No, there will be no hanging out. I need to figure out how to work next to him, and that's it."

The girls all exchange a look, and I know they want to argue with me, but I hold my hand up. "Please, let it be. I can't be a second-place person because he can't find Billie, and I can't live hoping he will remember what we had. He will never remember me, and I don't need false hope."

"But—" Piper began.

"Please. Don't."

She lets out a big breath and nods.

"There is no future for Xander and me besides as work colleagues." As I say it, I tell myself it's the truth, but it doesn't make it any less painful.

5

Xander

Five Months Earlier

"Come on. We're taking you out," Noah insists.

"No offense, but I'm not really in the going-out mood," I tell him.

It's been a month since I woke up in the hospital. Part of me wishes I'd have just stayed asleep or died in the accident.

Everything is confusing and frustrating. Noah, Jamison, Chase...they all tell me I'm not twenty-two. It's twelve years later. I'm no longer a paramedic. I've gone through med school and am a surgeon. According to Noah, I invested in several companies with him and am pretty wealthy. My apartment is fancier than I ever thought possible. And I am no longer with the love of my life, Billie.

Except I don't remember a single thing about the last twelve years, and every day that goes by, I lose more and more hope I'll ever get my memory back.

"Sorry, but I'm not letting you sit at home all night. Get dressed. You're coming out with us." Noah has his, *'I'm not letting you out of this,'* expression on, so I groan, go into the bathroom, and remove the pajama bottoms I've been wearing all day and take a shower.

When I walk out of my bedroom, Noah nods at me. "Good to see you can still clean up well."

"Funny. Good thing I didn't lose my good looks and amazing fashion sense in the accident." I joke about it, but I would have rather lost those things than my memory.

"What would all the ladies do if that had happened?" Noah teases me, but we both know I've not had any ass since before the accident. Any ass I got right before, I don't remember, so did it even happen? All I remember is screwing Billie since I was nineteen, in multiple positions and places, but she is nowhere.

To make things worse, a faceless woman haunts me every night, and it's not Billie, so I live in a constant state of guilt. I don't tell anyone about my dreams. I'm sure it's just my screwed-up mind playing more games on me. I never even had wet dreams this intense when I was a horny teenager, and the last thing I need to do is tell anyone about it and be deemed crazy.

"Let's get this over with," I mumble to Noah and snatch my keys off the table.

Noah's car and his driver Lou are waiting at the curb. That's another thing I can't seem to get used to. Noah, Jamison, and Chase have all changed. Yes, they are still the same guys I've always known, but they all have lives...stories I don't know. The last I knew, we were all paramedics. Now, Noah runs one of the largest merger and acquisition firms in the country and is worth billions. Jamison and Chase own ambulance companies in several states and are expanding. And my investment portfolio has more zeros behind it than I could have ever dreamed.

Apparently, the three of us were smart and gave whatever we could to Noah to invest in various companies and are all self-made billionaires.

I mean, seriously, how do four guys who scrambled for scraps become not millionaires but billionaires?

I thought Noah was playing a joke on me when he sat me down and said, "We need to go through your finances so you pay your bills on time and don't screw up your credit."

"Am I going to lose everything since I can't work right now?" I asked him seriously.

Noah laughed but then seemed to realize I was freaking out. "Xander, you're loaded. You never have to work again if you don't want to."

"Funny. Just give it to me straight. How long until I have to beg my parents to move back in with them? I'm sure my salary was nice and all, but with my student loans and no paycheck coming in, I'm sure this apartment will need to go."

Noah searched my eyes, not saying anything.

"It's okay. Don't sugarcoat it. I can handle it. How bad is it?"

"Xander, I'm not joking. We've done well. Really well. You invested in some of my first projects with me. You only work because you love being a surgeon. It would take a lot for you to run out of money."

"Stop being cruel. Just give it to me straight, Noah. How long?"

He gazed at me a minute, went over to my pile of unopened mail, sorted through it, and came back with about ten envelopes from different banks and financial firms. Throwing them on the table, he said, "Open them."

Slowly, I opened them. One statement after another confirmed he was telling the truth about my financial situation. When I had them all laid out in front of me, I added it up in my head and sat back in shock. "So I'm rich?"

Noah laughed. "Yep. Filthy fucking rich."

I tried to comprehend it.

I should have felt elated.

I should have been dancing on the table.

I should have been grateful I would not lose my fancy apartment and have to move in with my parents.

I felt nothing but more confusion.

What I last remember is buying ramen noodles and my mom bringing casserole dishes of lasagna to the station so the guys and I could eat something decent between our shifts and school studies.

How did it all happen? I wish I could comprehend it all, but I can't. I don't remember any of it.

Even my cell phone is so complicated, I hardly use it. What happened to my flip phone and paramedic beeper?

"Earth to Xander." Noah waves at me in the car.

"Oh, sorry," I mumble.

"Xander, you've got to snap out of it. You can't go down this hole," Noah says.

I glare at him. "Easy for you to say. You remember the last twelve years of your life. Mine, too, apparently."

"That may be true, but you didn't let me go down the hole when Nathan died, and I will not let you go down it."

Nathan. I turn toward the window, blinking back tears. Noah's brother died, and I can't remember that, either.

Noah's voice gets softer. "Xander, your memory will come back. Give it more time."

I stare out the window. "Will it? I'm beginning to think not."

"It will. I know it will."

I say nothing, and we soon pull up to the curb. When we get inside, Chase and Jamison are at the bar.

"Xander," they both call out.

They sound the same as they always have when they are at the bar and drinking, so I plunge into a false sense of comfort. Within minutes of our arrival, Chase orders shots, and I pound a few back. I haven't drunk alcohol in...well, I don't remember when. It doesn't take long before I feel buzzed and am smiling.

The hostess comes and tells us our table is ready. We grab our beers and sit down at the table. For the first time in a long time, I'm having fun. The guys and I spend dinner laughing.

I keep ordering more shots and am feeling pretty drunk. Noah says, "Think it's time to cut back on those."

I roll my eyes at him. "Don't be a wuss."

He laughs.

The waitress quickly comes back with the shots.

"No wuss zone. Drink up, Parker," Jamison says to Noah and then clinks my glass to his.

I throw back the shot. Then I notice the woman with honey-colored hair. She looks like her, and my pulse creeps up.

I stand up quickly, knocking over my chair and take a few steps. I grasp the back of her shoulder. "Billie?"

The woman turns around. She isn't Billie.

"I'm so sorry. I thought you were someone else."

She bats her eyes at me and smiles. "That's okay."

I sulk back to the table. "Shit. I will never find her."

"Stop searching for her. You're not with her. You don't want her," Chase says.

I glare at him. "Don't tell me what I want or don't want."

He's about to say something else when the staff in the restaurant start singing "Happy Birthday," and a cake with the number thirty-five on it is placed in front of me.

How the hell am I thirty-five?

The candles are flickering, and the guys are singing along with the staff when all the anger, frustration, confusion, and desperation I've felt the last month comes to the surface. I pick up my pint of beer and dump it on top of the cake.

The staff stops singing.

"Have you lost your mind, Xander?" Chase stands up quickly as the beer drips off the table and onto his pants.

"Yeah, motherfucker, I have lost my mind, in case you haven't been paying attention," I yell at him.

"Get a grip, man," Chase yells back.

I land a punch right in the middle of his nose. He steps back for a minute then comes back at me, and his fist collides with the side of my chin.

There is a ton of commotion and loud noise as people scream. Noah and Jamison are dragging us away from each other, and Chase and I are yelling.

Within minutes, the cops are in the restaurant, and Chase and I are being pulled out to the back alley. Jamison follows, and Noah is nowhere to be seen.

When we get outside, one cop demands, "What are you two thinking?"

"It's just a misunderstanding among friends, Simon," Chase mutters.

"It will kill me to arrest you two. You better hope Noah can clean up your mess," the other cop says.

They seem like they know us, but I've never seen them before. I glance at Jamison for answers.

"Crandle, can I talk to you a minute?"

The cop named Crandle and Jamison step away, leaving Chase, Simon, and myself.

"Xander, you could be in massive trouble with the medical board for this. What are you thinking, throwing punches in a restaurant?" Simon asks.

"I'm sorry, but do I know you?"

Simon peers at me. "Funny."

"Simon, he doesn't know who you are," Chase says with blood all over his face.

Simon looks over at Chase, then me, then back at Chase.

"It's true. Xander has amnesia from a car accident he was in a month ago."

Simon's head jerks to me. "Xander, man, I'm sorry to hear that. You doing okay?"

I stare at him, feeling like a pathetic loser once again. "I'm sorry, but I don't know you."

Pity crosses his face. It's an expression I've gotten to see on too many people's faces the last month. He pats me on the back. If my hands weren't cuffed behind me, I would punch him in the face.

Jamison and Crandle return just as Noah comes outside with another man I don't know.

"I won't press charges," the man says. "We've handled the matter privately. Please have them leave through the alley though. I don't need my customers thinking people can get away with that kind of behavior."

"I'm sorry," I say to him right away, feeling guilty I created a mess in his place of business.

He gives me a sympathetic expression. "You're forgiven, Xander. I hope your memory comes back quickly, man."

Once again, another person knows me, and I have no clue who they are.

The cops finally unfasten our handcuffs. Sobered up by now, I turn to Chase. "I'm sorry."

He nods. "Already forgiven, but next time, can you not hit my face? I think I'm going to need a nose job."

The four of us laugh, and I'm reminded that, as depressing as it's been, I still have things in my life to be grateful for, like these guys. Maybe I shouldn't kill myself after all.

6

Xander

Present Day

NOAH AND I HAVE A FEW BEERS AND DINNER TOGETHER. HE SAID Piper is out with the girls, and I almost ask him where. The thought crosses my mind to go there and make Charlotte talk to me, but I don't ask.

It's after eight when I get to the hotel. My thoughts aren't any less messy than before, except now I'm confused about my feelings for Billie and what I felt with Charlotte earlier.

If only I could remember. How many times have I said that over the last six months? Why can't I remember?

I pull at my hair as I step inside my hotel room. After a quick shower, I lie in bed and replay the day and my conversation with Noah.

Then it hits me. Noah told me he thought Charlotte and I texted a lot.

I pull out my phone and type the name Charlotte in. Hundreds of messages pop up. I scroll, and, after fifteen minutes, I get to the very top of our text conversations. For the next few hours, I read through everything, with various emotions popping up.

A few texts make me laugh. Some make me sad. Most make me feel wanted.

She's sweet.

She's funny.

She's raw and honest.

Over the next few hours, I learn a lot about Charlotte...and myself.

It's very clear Charlotte wasn't pursuing me. I may not remember everything, but reading these messages, I'm 100 percent obsessed with this girl. I initiated most of the conversations. I've pursued her. Not a day goes by from the first text message to the day before the accident that I didn't begin several conversations with her. From the time I got up until I went to bed, she was all I thought about, based on my text messages to her.

"Good morning, gorgeous. Did you sleep well? Sorry I kept you up so late on the phone." Okay, so we were talking on the phone as well, like Noah said.

"You should have seen the crazy-ass cyst I removed from this guy's femur today. You would have loved all the extra pus." She sent me back heart emojis. What other girl could I ever joke around with about this kind of stuff humor? Who enjoyed my warped sense of humor?

Not Billie runs through my mind.

"Send me a picture of you."

She sent me a picture, blowing me a kiss. She's so damn gorgeous.

"What are you wearing?"

She sent me a picture of her in her red lace bra, but only the back of it, not the front. *Fuck, that's hot.*

"Did you get home safely?" When she wrote back yes, I told her I was FaceTiming her.

"Club D sucked. I kept wishing you were here with me. When I get to Chicago, I'm taking you out." I was making long-term plans with her.

"Can you send me Vivian's number so I can view apartments when I'm there? Do you want to come with me, so I don't end up in a crappy bachelor pad you hate to stay over in?" She teased me about being presumptuous, and I told her all the ways I would make her cum when I saw her next.

"You're getting extra dessert for paying over three grand for me." I still can't believe she paid that much money so another girl didn't get a date with me. And she did it over the phone.

"You should come to New York and surprise me." That was the night before she flew out to New York and surprised me.

"I miss you." I lost track of the number of times I had texted her that. And I had only been with her one night when I started sending her those messages.

There is no way I would have ever sent all these messages unless I was head over heels for this girl. And I understand why from all her messages.

No wonder she's heartbroken. I destroyed her. I destroyed us.

I save several pictures she sent me to me and realize I already had saved them. I just hadn't opened the gallery on my phone since the accident.

Staring at her picture, I see the lips and hair that have been in my dreams all these months. It's complete now. There is no more faceless woman. And damn if she isn't the most beautiful creature I've ever seen.

Guilt crashes through me as Billie's image pops up in my mind. I throw my phone on the bed and put my hands over my face, trying to remember anything new, but nothing comes. It's the same memories as always.

Billie's face, clear in my mind as she laughs and kisses me.

Noah wouldn't lie to me, and if he says Billie and I split and weren't happy, then we must not have been, but I can't understand or accept it until I remember it.

But now I also have Charlotte's face popping up. Her tear-filled eyes are ripping my heart out, and the picture she sent smiling and blowing me a kiss is rotating in my mind.

Rationality tells me I shouldn't feel guilty about thinking about Charlotte instead of Billie, but it's a tug-of-war in my mind.

Did I really fall out of love with Billie? I still can't fathom it. But do I love two women, even if I only was with one a very short time.

Is it possible to love two people at once?

It's past ten now, and I have to be at the hospital at four in the morning for surgery. I should go to sleep. Instead, I pull up Charlotte's number.

I text her. "Are you awake?"

I wait, about to assume she's asleep when I finally get a reply. "Yes."

Without thinking, I hit the FaceTime button.

Xander, what are you doing?

It rings and rings, and I think it is about to stop ringing when she picks up. She is silent

"Hey," I say.

She slowly waves.

"I just spent the last few hours reading our text messages."

Her eyes widen. "Okay..."

I take a deep breath. "Look, I don't know what I'm doing right now. I'm not sure why I can't remember things. I know what people tell me, and it just doesn't make sense because I can't remember any of it." I pull at my hair in frustration.

"Xander, are you okay?"

Tears well up in my eyes, and I gaze up at the ceiling. "No. I'm not. I just spent the last few hours getting a glimpse into us, and I don't remember you. Except for my dreams...every single night, you haunt my dreams. But I can't remember a goddamn thing about you...about us. And I'm sorry. I'm so sorry. You don't deserve it."

"It's okay. I'm not mad at you. You don't need to feel guilty about anything. It's my fault this happened, so I should be the one to apologize."

"Your fault?"

She nods. "If I hadn't surprised you and let you drive me to the airport, none of this would have happened."

"That wasn't your fault."

"Yes, it was."

"No, it wasn't. It's no one's fault. But if you want to blame someone, blame me. Go read the text messages. I told you to come surprise me."

"I should have just taken a taxi."

"Stop it. It was an accident. And I'm so sorry I hurt you. It's tearing me up right now, and I hate myself for it."

She looks away and then back at me. "Xander, you've done nothing wrong. It's okay. Just let it go and don't think about it anymore. It is what it is."

"No, Charlotte. You don't understand what I'm trying to tell you."

"What are you trying to tell me?"

"Everyone around me can tell me how things were or what I should or shouldn't feel, but I know myself. I know what I felt when I saw you today. I know what I felt when I read all those messages. I know myself, and I can't ignore what's in those messages."

Charlotte takes a big breath. "What's that?"

"A man who's crazy about a woman he only met a few times."

She blinks back tears and bites her lip. "But you don't remember me?"

I shake my head. "Only in my dreams."

"But you still love Billie?"

I rub my hands in my face. "Yes. No. I don't know. I know what I remember. I hear what Noah, Chase, and Jamison tell me. I'm trying to wrap my head around it but without the memories, it makes it hard for me not to feel for her what I last remember."

A pained expression crosses Charlotte's face.

"I'm sorry. I don't want to lie to you."

"Okay."

"Charlotte, I know I have feelings for you. I felt them today when I saw you. I didn't understand though. Then I read our messages."

She closes her eyes and turns away.

"Charlotte."

She slowly faces me then opens her eyes. "What do you want from me, Xander?"

"I don't know. I didn't have a plan when I asked you if you were awake."

She laughs softly. "Fair enough."

"You have a nice laugh and smile," I blurt out.

She smiles a little bigger then yawns.

"Are you at the hospital tomorrow?"

"I have to be there around four."

I laugh. "Me, too."

"I bet money we are in the same surgery."

"I would be okay with that. Would you?"

She pauses for a moment. "Yeah. I'd be okay with that."

"Good. I'm going to let you get some sleep now. I'll see you in a few hours."

She smiles. "All right. Hey, Xander?"

"Yeah."

"Thanks for calling."

I wink at her. "Thanks for taking my call."

7

Charlotte

Nine Months Earlier

I'm curled in Xander's arms when my phone buzzes. I crawl over him to pick my phone up off the table then snuggle back into him.

He wakes up and yawns. "Everything okay?"

I pull open my messages. An unknown number is on the screen. I pop my code into the phone and read the message that also has Vivian and Quinn's names on it. "It's Piper. Does one of you have my phone?"

"Vivian has it," I type just as Quinn and Vivian respond as well.

I show Xander. "I'm assuming this is Noah's number?"

He glances at it. "Looks like it."

I save the number under Noah.

Xander snatches my phone.

"What are you doing?"

"Making sure I have your number." He grins at me, sends himself a text message from my phone, then programs his number in.

"I already told you I'd give it to you."

He's about to hand my phone back to me when a YouTube notification comes across it. He swipes the announcement, and a video of a doctor removing a cyst pops up.

"So, you really do love this stuff." He grins at me.

"Yep. I get sucked into it."

"You are seriously the hottest girl I've ever met, in so many ways."

My cheeks heat.

We watch a few minutes of the video, commenting on things and laughing until he throws the phone on the bed and turns into me, resting his face on his elbow. "Do you ever go to New York?"

"Only once. I went with the girls to Times Square for New Year's Eve."

He rolls his eyes. "That is not the way to experience New York."

"It was okay. I take it you don't like drunks throwing up and peeing in the streets?"

"I always hated New Year's Eve. The ambulance could hardly move."

"Surgeons go in ambulances? Is that a New York thing?"

He strokes my hip. "No. Noah and I were paramedics. It's how we paid for school."

I jerk back in shock. "Really?"

"Yep."

"Wow. That must have been a crazy schedule."

He shrugs. "It was worth it."

"So you were a paramedic and in med school. How is that even possible? Did you ever sleep?"

He grins. "I can run on very little."

"So, when you leave my place, you won't go crash at Noah's?"

"Probably not. Speaking of Noah, what's up with him and Piper?"

"Honestly, no clue. She said he's an asshole. Is he?"

Xander shakes his head. "Not that I'm aware of. Noah said she hates him?"

"She didn't act like she did."

"Sounds messed up to me," he comments.

"You said you move in a few months?"

"Probably four. Dr. Richardson hasn't set his retirement date yet."

"Dr. Richardson is who you're taking over for?"

"Yeah, you know him?"

"I do. I assist him in his surgeries."

Xander's face brightens. "So, we might get to work together?"

"Probably."

He licks his lips. "I guess I have even more to look forward to when I move to Chicago."

I laugh as Xander's phone buzzes.

He groans. "Ten bucks, that's Noah." Reading his phone, he puts his forehead on my chest, groaning again.

I kiss his forehead. "What's so horrible?"

"Noah wants to meet up for breakfast. Piper slipped out on him. He's freaking."

I run my hand through his hair, disappointed he has to leave, but I put a smile on my face. "Sounds like he needs a friend right now."

Xander picks his head up and kisses me. "He can wait," he murmurs, and I once again get lost in a perfect storm of Xander and Charlotte.

————

I GET A TEXT FROM XANDER LATER THAT DAY. "NOAH'S A RIGHT mess."

"What happened? Piper isn't answering our calls or text messages."

"She told Noah she has a hot date tonight and to stop bothering her."

I roll my eyes and feel bad for Noah. "I am 99 percent sure that Piper does not have a date. Tell Noah to chill. She's just trying to get under his skin."

"Mission accomplished," Xander writes back.

I send some crying emojis.

Xander sends a GIF of a knife stabbing a heart.

I text Piper. "You need to respond to us. What is going on?"

Xander sends me another text. "It appears I'm on friend duty all night. I want to see you before I go back. Can I take you to breakfast, or brunch, or whatever people do in Chicago on a Sunday?"

Excitement shoots through me, and it's replaced with disappointment when I remember I have to work. "Sorry, I'm in surgery all day tomorrow. I won't finish until two or possibly even four."

Minutes go by then he responds, "Bummer. My flight leaves at four thirty. What time do you start work?"

"Four."

"Early day. So what time do you leave your place to get to work by four? Just wondering for future reference."

"Around three thirty."

"Good to know. Noah's freaking out again, so I have to go."

"Have fun."

He sends me a kiss emoji.

I send him one back.

I want to see Xander again. It sounds like the only way I'll get to before he goes is if Piper answers her phone, and we can all somehow meet up. I call Piper again, but it goes to voice mail.

Damn it. I really like this guy, and four months will be a long time to wait.

———

IT's 3:25 A.M. ON SUNDAY, AND MY PHONE RINGS. XANDER'S NAME pops up on the screen.

Why is he calling me this early?

"Hey, is everything okay?" I answer.

"Your chariot awaits," he says.

"My chariot?"

He laughs. "When you're ready, come down. I'm in the black car outside your front door."

I go to the window and peer down. It's pitch-black except for the street lights, but I faintly make out a car sitting at the curb.

"You're waiting for me?"

"Yep. Come down."

"I'll be there in a few minutes I just need to finish getting ready."

"No problem. See you soon."

My heart beats faster, and I look in the mirror. My hair is in a bun for work, and I pull it out and try to make it nicer, securing the hair tie over my wrist for later.

A million thoughts are racing through my mind.

He came to see me again.

Is he seriously in the car?

Is this really happening?

Who is this guy?

Within minutes, I'm outside, and he steps out of the back of the car. He wraps me in his arms and kisses me. "Good morning."

"Good morning. I didn't expect to see you again so soon. And especially not this early."

"I told you I wanted to see you before I left."

I'm smiling so big my face is hurting. "Well, it's nice to see you again."

He steps back, opens the door, and motions for me to get in.

Is this guy for real?

I get into the car, and he follows. The dividing window is closed.

"How do you take your coffee?" He opens a brown paper bag. I notice two cups in the holder.

"Cream, two sugars, not the fake crap."

He mixes them into my cup, puts the lid back on, then adds the stopper to it. In one swift move, he pulls me onto his lap.

"You're crazy," I tell him.

"Crazy about you."

My face flushes.

"Do you have a busy day?" he asks.

"Probably. I don't know the full schedule until I get in."

He nods.

"Did you get any sleep?" The back of my fingers graze his cheek.

He chuckles softly. "Nope."

"You stayed up all night to surprise me?"

A cocky grin of pride floods his face. "Yep."

I lean in and kiss him. He wraps his arms around me, as I part his lips with mine, slipping my tongue next to his. Flutters erupt in every cell of my body, and he pulls me in tighter against him.

"Thank you," I murmur against his lips. "This is the sweetest thing anyone has ever done for me."

"Really?"

"Yes."

I lace my hands behind his head and melt into him, knowing in my heart he is special, different from all the other men who have ever been in my life, and that I want to see more of him.

We make out the entire way to my work. When the car stops, I don't notice until the driver opens the door.

I pull back in surprise.

Xander looks at the driver. "Give us a minute, please."

The driver nods and closes the door.

Xander pushes my hair back from my face. "I'll text you his number. Text him ten minutes before you're ready to leave, and he will drive you home."

"I can get an Uber or cab," I tell him quickly.

"No way. The driver will take you home. It's already arranged."

"All right. Thank you."

He kisses me again.

I sigh. "I have to go or I'll be late."

He pecks me on the lips. "I'll talk to you soon, okay?"

I take the coffee from the cup holder. "Okay. Thanks for this and the ride."

He winks at me. "Anytime."

When I turn to go, he spins me back around and kisses me so passionately, my knees would buckle if I wasn't seated.

"Don't forget me."

"I won't."

He pecks me one last time and I go into work. Inside the locker room, I run into Damon, my ex, who scowls at me. I ignore him and go about my business but can't help feeling his scrutiny.

As quick as I can, I get ready, grab my coffee, and read the schedule. I leave the locker room and Damon's nasty glares then head off to my first surgery.

I spend the day in several operations, trying to concentrate and not think about Xander, but it's tough. He's in my mind, and I can't get him out.

When I'm done with my shift, I go to my locker and pull out my phone. He has texted me the driver's number, and I notify the driver what time to pick me up.

The car is sitting at the curb when I step outside. The driver opens the door and I get in. On the seat is a massive bouquet of pink roses and a note.

I open the envelope.

CHARLOTTE,

Don't forget me.

XOXO,

Xander

PS - I miss you already.

FORGET ABOUT HIM? AS IF THAT WOULD EVER BE POSSIBLE.

I glance at the time on my phone and know he's on his plane, already in the air. I send him a text. "Don't forget me. And I miss you, too."

8

Xander

Eight Months Earlier

MY FLIGHT JUST LANDED IN COLUMBUS, OHIO. I REMOVE MY suitcase from the overhead bin and make my way off the plane and through the airport.

The air is warmer than it usually is in May, and the cab driver has all the windows rolled down.

"Hyatt Regency, please," I tell him.

"You in town for the medical convention?" he asks.

"Yes."

"You're arriving late. Most of the doctors came in yesterday."

"I was in surgery all day yesterday."

Plus, I had to rearrange my entire schedule over the next two days.

We continue to chat until we get to the hotel. I quickly check in, take a quick shower then open the pamphlet the registration lady gave me regarding the conference.

I scan through it and find the breakout session I want to attend.

If I go now, I'll catch the last fifteen minutes.

I throw on the lanyard with the conference badge I also received at check-in and quickly maneuver through the hotel and conference room.

When I enter the session, Charlotte is at the front of the room, using the laser to point out different pus pockets that can occur from orthopedic surgery.

I slide into a seat in the back of the room.

The conference is for doctors going through their residency. I'm way beyond that and would never be at it.

But she is here.

Yesterday, Charlotte texted me. "Guess who gets to spend three days in Columbus for two presentations."

"How did that happen?"

"The regional is sick, and they said I know it best."

"Who is it for?"

"Residents."

I replied, "When do you leave?"

"My flight leaves at noon."

"Staying until Wednesday?"

"Yes."

"I haven't been to Columbus, but I heard it's fun," I texted, as I went over my schedule for the next few days in my head.

"I'm sure it's great. Guess I'll have lots of time to sightsee."

All I've been dying to do over the last month is see her again. So I figured out how to get out of work on Tuesday and Wednesday, paid the thousand dollar conference fee, and booked the first flight out and hotel room.

We've spent the last month texting, emailing, calling, and seeing each other on FaceTime, but our schedules have been crazy, and I miss her. And she also paid three grand for me in a charity auction over FaceTime.

What girl does something that awesome?

I only saw Charlotte once. Well, twice if you count a fifteen-minute car ride to drop her off at work. Seeing her in the flesh has my pants in a stir. She's the most gorgeous woman on earth, I thought when I met her, and she's living up to that theory today. Her long, blonde hair she's wearing straight. The clearest blue eyes I've ever seen are shining bright, and her pink lips are just as inviting as ever. The blue pencil skirt hugs her hips just the right way, showing off her killer calves, and the button up, form-fitting yellow top reminds me of sunshine.

That's what she is. Sunshine.

And I knew she was smart, but watching her present reiterates how intelligent she really is. She's leaps ahead of any medical device rep that I've had assist me in surgery.

At the end of her presentation, she asks if there are questions. I let the residents ask, and when there seems to be no more, I sit up straighter in my chair and hold my hand up.

She points in my direction. "Yes."

I stand up. "What do you rate the pus factor in slide 28?"

Surprise passes her face. Then a big grin takes over. A faint blush creeps up her neck. "From my experience, I'd give it an eight point three."

My eyes don't leave hers. "Hmm. You've seen worse than that?"

"A few stand out in my mind."

"What about the smell factor?"

Her smile grows wider. "Too hard to tell by pictures. You never know until you're fully in there, but judging by the color, I'm assuming it isn't as bad as it appears."

The administrator rings a bell. "Sorry to cut you off, doctor, but it's time for the general session," a woman's voice says. I don't know what she looks like, as I'm still staring at Charlotte.

The doctors trail out of the room, and I stay in my spot as a few residents form a line to ask Charlotte questions. When it's just us, I close the door, lock it, and head to the front of the room.

Charlotte meets me halfway. "I can't believe... What are you doing here?"

I lace both my hands in her hair and tilt her head back. Dipping down, I part her lips with my tongue and roll it around her delicious mouth.

Her fingers grip my hair, and she pulls me closer, deepening our kiss.

I put my palm on her back. "Tell me you still feel our heat."

"Smoldering," she breathes.

"I missed you."

"What are you doing here?" she repeats.

I continuing kissing her. "I thought three grand deserved two dates."

"Two, huh?"

"Mm-hmm. One in New York and one in Columbus."

"Columbus, huh?"

"Yep. We'll figure New York out," I promise.

Someone bangs on the door, and we pull back "I guess I shouldn't lock people out." I wink at her and open the door.

A woman is standing in the hall. "Oh, sorry, Dr."—she glances at my badge—"Dr. Kane. I didn't mean to interrupt?"

"No problem, the door must have accidentally locked. I was just trying to get more information from Ms. DeVoe."

Charlotte joins me with her laptop bag on her shoulder and her purse.

"Thank you again for presenting at the last minute. Do you need anything else in the room for tomorrow?" the woman whose name badge says Kayla asks.

Charlotte tilts her head, considering. "Everything was perfect. I'll see you tomorrow?"

"Sure. But we hope you'll join us at the happy hour for presenters tonight at six in the main bar of the Hyatt."

"Okay. Thank you."

We say our goodbyes, and when we get to the escalator, I grab Charlotte's laptop bag.

"What are you doing?"

"Carrying your bag."

She laughs. "Aren't you chivalrous."

"You're done for the day, right?" I ask her.

"Yep. Two o'clock tomorrow is my next commitment."

"So, I get you till then?"

"If you want me till then, yes."

I slide my arm around her waist. "Is that really a question?"

"So where are we going?" she asks.

"To my room so I can show you how much I've missed you." I cockily lick my lips.

Her sexy blush creeps across her face again. "Have you missed me a little or a lot?"

I turn to her. "I've missed you more than I ever thought possible. I can't wait to get to Chicago so I can see more of you."

She rests her head on my shoulder. "Feeling is mutual."

I lean down and brush my lips across hers. "I'm taking you out for a proper date tonight, but you get your first serving of dessert before."

She giggles. "So, I'll be having lots of desserts today?"

I wink at her. "You will if I have anything to do with it."

We spend the next two days having multiple orgasms, exploring Columbus, and learning more about each other and all the things we have in common. Everything is easy and fun with Charlotte. She's real, honest, and the sweetest girl I've ever met. I'm more infatuated with her than before I left New York. When we have to part ways, the only thing I can think about is how to see her again soon.

9

Charlotte

Present Day

IT'S THREE IN THE MORNING, AND MY ALARM RINGS. I HAVE HAD little sleep, but I'm not overly tired.

Xander's text and phone call surprised me. When his name popped up on the screen, I froze and quickly debated about texting him back. Then he FaceTimed me.

My heart broke again, seeing tears in his eyes as he struggles with his amnesia. He's having a hard time, which is understandable, but a big part of his frustration is now me. He told me he read our messages...messages I've spent too many hours to count rereading. He claims he feels something for me.

I curse myself for the resurgence of hope. *Pull it together, Charlotte. He doesn't remember you, and he's still in love with Billie.*

I get ready and head for the hospital. Before I can even contemplate what I'm doing, I text Xander.

"I don't know what hotel you're at, but do you want me to pick you up?"

"I'm at the Claybourne. Is it on the way?"

"Yes."

"Sure. That would be awesome. Thanks."

What am I doing?

As much as I reprimand myself for putting myself in the position to be hurt further, I can't help but feel excited.

I hope it isn't weird being in a car so close to him.

What am I doing?

I pull up to the doors of the hotel, and Xander is already waiting outside with a black wool cap on and holding two cups of coffee. I hadn't seen him in a hat before, and he looks straight out of a magazine ad.

As he opens the door and gets in, his sexy scent flares in my nostrils. He sets the coffee in my cup holders, leans over, and kisses me on the cheek. "Good morning."

I freeze.

He freezes. "Hey, I'm sorry. I didn't think before I did that."

"It's okay. There are worse things you could do to me."

"I realize I lost my memory, but let's hope I don't go down that path."

I laugh and pull the car out.

"Thanks for picking me up."

"Sure. You look hot in that hat." Shit! My face flushes.

"Thanks. I'll have to wear it more often."

I try to concentrate on the road.

"I took a chance and listened to my gut. It told me you take your coffee with cream and two sugars, but real sugar, not that fake crap."

"Xander! You remembered! That's great!"

He throws his arm in the air for a victory pump. "There's hope for me yet."

"There's always hope. I learned that as a kid." I focus on the road.

"You mean because of the orphanage?" Xander says quietly.

I jerk my head at him. "You remember that?"

"No. I read it in our text messages."

My heart falls in disappointment. "Thanks for the coffee," I say quickly, not wanting to talk anymore about my childhood.

Xander blessedly changes the subject. "So, how often do you get to pick the music in the OR?"

I glance over at him. "Not a fan of Club Hip Hop Radio?"

He laughs. "I am. I was hoping we could listen to it again today, or something else besides Dr. Croy's fifties channel. The last week, before you were back, I thought I would go crazy."

Rolling my eyes, I tell him, "One week is nothing. I had to endure two years before I won a bet, and now he has to play rock, paper, scissors with me."

Xander groans. "I would transfer units if I had to endure two years."

"It was torture for sure."

"So, what was the bet?"

"That green pus instead of yellow would come out of the patient's knee."

Xander laughs. "That's awesome."

"Yep, it was," I agree. "He also had to buy me blueberry muffins from the lobby every day for a month."

"Blueberry muffins?"

"Yep. They make these mini ones, and they're beyond delicious."

"Well, I hope you win rock, paper, scissors today."

"I hope so, too."

"Did you get any sleep?" Xander asks.

"A little. You?"

"Same."

"Did you dream about me?" I tease, then realize what I said. "Shit. I'm sorry." Heat blazes across my face.

"As a matter of fact, I did."

My face flushes further.

"At least you weren't faceless this time."

"Faceless?"

"You've been faceless all these months."

"Then how do you know it was me?"

Xander blurts out, "Because I could smell, feel, taste, hear, and see all of you except your face."

"You could taste me? Jeez, what were you doing to me," I say, once again not thinking, then put my hand on my face in embarrassment. "Shit. I don't know what's wrong with my mouth today. Just ignore me."

Xander laughs. "I think we both have that problem. Why don't we stop saying we are sorry and not worry about it?"

I glance over at him. "Okay. No more sorry."

"And I'm doing everything possible to you. That's how I taste you," he states.

My lower body pulses at the thought.

"In last night's dream, we were in a shower. Am I creating scenarios in my head, or did that happen?"

My face is officially on fire. I glance over at Xander, and he has a cocky grin on his face. "It happened," I say and focus back at the road.

"You're pretty adorable when you blush," Xander says.

My heart is racing, and my stomach flutters. *Simmer down, Charlotte. The guy is just having flashbacks.*

Life is so not fair.

"Since you didn't taste me yesterday in surgery, how did you know it was me?" I tease him but also want to know.

"I smelled you when you stood by me. Then you pulled your hair cap off and said my name. You only say my name in my dreams."

Eyes on the road, Charlotte.

I'm sitting in a car, next to the man I want to be with but can't, while he tells me he's having dreams of us having sex. *This is so fucked-up.*

"So you dated Damon?" Xander asks in another change of subject but not one I welcome.

"Yeah. I broke up with him the week before I met you."

Xander shifts in his seat.

"What?" I glance over at him.

He shrugs and raises an eyebrow.

"What does that mean?"

"I don't see you with a guy like that."

"A guy like that?"

"Arrogant, moody, full of himself...should I keep going?"

I'm not sure why I stick up for Damon, but I do. "He wasn't like that when we dated."

"No?"

To the best of my memory he wasn't. "I don't think he was like that to others, either, when we were together." *Well, at least when we dated. After is a different story.*

"Really? That's not what the others say."

Jeez. What did Damon do all these months to make everyone hate him so much? He can be a jerk but I don't recall him being one at work.

"Well, he wasn't like that," I say quietly.

"Sorry, I shouldn't talk bad about your ex."

"It's okay."

"Did you love him?" Xander blurts out.

Did I love him? *No, but I fell in love with you.*

I quietly say, "No."

"Sorry. I shouldn't pry."

"I thought we weren't apologizing anymore?"

"You're right. I'll still try not to pry into your life. I don't know why I feel like I can blurt anything out to you today."

"Probably because that's what we used to do," I reply. "Like that. I just did it without even thinking."

"Hmm."

"What does hmm mean?" I ask.

"I've never had anyone I could do that with before."

"Yeah, me, either," I say sadly and will myself not to stare at Xander.

The rest of the ride is quiet, but it isn't an uncomfortable silence. It's another stab to my heart about how good we are together. *Doesn't everyone want someone they can talk to about anything?*

I pull into the parking garage and find a spot. We step out of the car and stroll into the building, and when someone walks toward us, Xander rests his palm on the small of my back, like it's normal, letting me go ahead of him but staying close to me. I hold myself back from leaning into him more or turning around and wrapping my arms around him.

Ugh. Why do we still have to be so good together?

We get to the locker room, and someone is leaving, so Xander puts his hand on my back again and has me go through the door. We are almost to the lockers when Damon glances over at us. He scowls at Xander's hand, which is still on my back.

"Hey, Damon," I say nicely.

One dark eyebrow lifted. "Playing in the sandbox rather quickly, aren't you, Charlotte?"

I glare at him. "Excuse me?"

Xander pushes me back a bit and steps between me and Damon. "I suggest you keep your nose in your own business and stop talking about things you know nothing about."

Crap. This isn't good.

Damon steps closer, almost nose to nose with Xander. "Is that right?"

Xander moves in. "Yes. Do you have a problem with that?"

I'm about to say something when Dr. Sear comes around the corner from the other aisle of lockers. "You two can both cool it."

They glance at Dr. Sear but neither moves.

"Is something wrong with your ears? I said to cool it. That means, step back."

Xander obeys, continuing to stare at Damon who doesn't move.

"Damon, are you deaf?" Dr. Sear sternly asks him.

Damon glares at Xander. "We'll finish this later."

"No, you won't," Dr. Sear says.

Damon scowls. "Yeah, okay. Whatever you say."

Dr. Sear walks up to him. "Do you have a problem we should discuss in private?"

Damon purses his lips. "Nope. I'm good." He shoves his bag in the locker and leaves.

Dr. Sear turns toward me. "Charlotte, is he harassing you?"

I shake my head. "No, that was the first incident."

"If he does, I want to know."

"Okay. I'm sure it will be fine, but thank you."

Dr. Sear focuses on Xander. "I need you to use your head, or you're on the first flight out of here. We don't need any lawsuits."

Xander clenches his jaw.

"Do you understand me, Dr. Kane?"

"Yes."

"Good. I would hate to see that happen. You're an excellent surgeon, and I have big plans for you."

Xander goes over to his locker, and Dr. Sear goes back to his side of the locker room. I put my bag away. Xander is not happy, and I can tell.

Great. This is all he needs. More stress won't help his memory.

I want to tell him I'm sorry, but I don't want to with Dr. Sear around. I'm getting my scrubs and hair cap on for surgery when I finally catch Xander's eye. I mouth, "I'm sorry."

Xander mouths, "Not your fault," and gives me a panty-melting grin.

I read the operating list and see Xander and I are in the same surgery. "We're in operating room five."

Xander reads the list then draws a deep breath and lets it out. "Charlotte, please make sure you win rock, paper, scissors today."

10

Charlotte

Three Months Earlier

UNLOCKING THE DOOR TO MY APARTMENT, I STEP INSIDE AND glance around.

So much has changed, yet everything remains the same.

What did I expect?

I sigh and roll the different-colored suitcases inside.

You left with a carry-on and came back with more baggage...lots of baggage.

For the millionth time, Xander's face pops into my mind. I curse myself again, but no matter how often I do, it doesn't stop the ache in my heart or the constant reel playing in my head about Xander.

My foot has been healing over the last several months, and I finally got a walking cast. The first chance I had to leave New York, I did. Piper and Noah were more than gracious hosts, but I assumed if I could get out of the city where Xander was, it would be easier to forget about him.

But I can't. He was only in my apartment one time, but he's everywhere. He's in my kitchen and sitting on my barstool. He's in my shower and bed. Then I notice, taped to my fridge, all the notes from the flowers he sent me every week.

The notes always say, "Don't forget me," and how much he misses me.

Don't forget me. Isn't that a cruel joke?

Through angry tears, I tear the notes off the fridge. I try not to blame him for our situation because he has amnesia, and it's not his fault, but at this moment, I wish I could hate him.

But I can't.

I take all the note cards and consider throwing them out, but I stop myself. The lid of the trash can is open, and I'm about to drop them in, but I can't do it. Instead, I open an empty drawer and put them in there.

I spend the day dusting my apartment. When I left for New York, it was the beginning of summer, and now it's fall. Bored, I turn on the television and get sucked into a deeper depression, watching Lifetime and Hallmark channel movies, imagining all the things I would do with Xander had the accident not happened.

I'm halfway through a box of Kleenex when my phone vibrates. I pick it up to find a Words with Friends notification that NYSurgeon has made a move.

My pulse increases, and my stomach flips. Xander. Does he remember?

Hope creeps up, and I read the board. "Contusion," he wrote.

I can't help myself and open the chat box. "Nice one."

I'm studying the board, seeing what word I can write when the chat box blinks I have a message. I hold my breath and open it. "Guess I had enough time to figure it out. Sorry it took so long. I got a notification I was behind. I don't use my phone much these days."

He still doesn't remember. My gut drops, and I tell myself to delete the app, but instead, I torment myself further.

"It's okay. Things happen."

"Isn't that the cruel truth."

Right away, I respond, "Are you okay?"

A minute goes by. "I'm sorry. I'm having some memory issues. Do I know you?"

My heart bleeds more. I debate about telling him, but I finally write, "Only on here. You don't have to worry about anything you say. Think of this as a safe zone since you don't know me besides my awesome talent at medical term Scrabble."

"LOL. You do seem to be pretty good at this."

"I beat you quite a bit."

"Ouch."

"LOL...sorry, but not sorry?" We banter back and forth.

"So, where are you located?" Xander writes.

I almost write Chicago but put, "The Midwest."

"That's why you're so nice!"

"So they say. You must be from New York based on your user ID."

"Yes."

For months, I told Piper not to talk to me about Xander, but it's killing me, not knowing how he's doing. I type, "Is it hard not remembering things?"

"You want the answer I give everyone or the honest one?"

"The honest one."

"What's hard is other people telling you what you should or shouldn't feel. They don't get it. If you aren't in my shoes, you can't understand it."

"Go on," I tell him, just to torture myself more.

"Your memories all have feelings attached to them. So if you can't remember something, it doesn't matter how many times someone tells you what happened and how you felt."

Tears fall, as I know he's talking about Billie, but I keep chatting with him.

"That makes sense," I write because it's the truth. I understand his rationale.

"My memories are coming back, but it's in waves, and it's like my brain is a mishmash of puzzle pieces with too many holes."

"That must be difficult."

"I won't lie. It got pretty dark a month ago."

My pulse creeps up. "What do you mean?"

He doesn't write back. After ten minutes, I try again, "I'm sorry if I pried too much."

"You didn't. I'm trying to figure out what to say without sounding pathetic."

"Don't worry about that."

"I fell into a bad depression. I wished I'd gotten killed in the accident or just not woken up."

More tears fall out of my eyes. "Do you still feel that way?"

"Not anymore. I'm remembering things. So I have hope again."

"Never give up. Even when it seems pointless, hope is always something to hold on to." I wonder if he remembers anything about me.

"I'm going to write that down. That's a good reminder for me."

I want to tell him who I am. To ask him if he remembers anything about me, but I don't.

"Hey, my buddy is here for our run. I need to go. Finish this game later?"

"Sure. Have a good run."

"Thanks for not judging me."

"I never will. You can throw whatever you want at me."

"Thanks. It's nice to talk to someone who doesn't know me."

A pain of guilt stabs me. Instead of confessing, I write, "Agree. Talk to you later."

I throw my phone on the couch and stare into space for a while, reflecting on everything Xander revealed.

No matter how much time goes by, I can't shake him, and having spoken with him, my love for him isn't any less than before. But now I'm worried about him and his mental state.

I spend the day with our conversation haunting me. When night-time comes, I get into bed, pull up the Words with Friends chat box, and reread the conversation.

I don't message him, but I take my next move on the board then put my phone on the table.

Within a few minutes, a notification pops up on my phone. We don't message each other but only play the game. At the end of the game, I place my final word on the board and beat him. A message pops up. "Nice game. Your medical vocabulary is extensive. Are you a doctor?"

I hesitate for a minute then decide to tell him the truth. "No, I'm a medical device rep and assist the doctors in surgery."

"Ah. That makes sense."

"How was your run?"

"Great. Want to play again?"

"Yes."

He begins another game, and we play several. We banter back and forth during each of the games, and I feel joy for the first time in months. At three in the morning, I'm yawning and having a hard time keeping my eyes open. "I need to get some sleep."

"Thanks for playing. This is the most fun I've had in a long time."

My heart lifts. "Me, too."

"Get some sleep. I'll work on upgrading my vocab to beat your ass next time."

"Sounds good. Sweet dreams."

"Night."

I put my phone on the table and wrap my arms around my pillow. My mind is racing with so many thoughts of Xander. We're still so good together.

I close my eyes. With mixed emotions, I fall asleep, only to have nightmares of our accident, and hear Xander moaning in pain.

And even though I'm aware it's bad for me, night after night, and sometimes during the day, I play Words with Friends with Xander, laughing and crying over our messages.

Xander

Present Day

TODAY IS A DAY OF NONCOMPLICATED SURGERIES. I HAVE THREE different operations. Charlotte and I are in the first two together.

Charlotte wins the rock, paper, scissors contest, and she chooses the nineties top hits channel. When she wins, I wink at her.

We work together well, side by side, and it's a fun day, until my last surgery.

The last one I have on my own, and Charlotte has two more with other surgeons. When I walk into the operating room for my final surgery, I have to maintain my cool.

Damon is over at the nurse's station, getting his gloves put on. I silently groan.

This guy is a complete asshole. He wasn't someone I wanted to make friends with before I learned he'd dated Charlotte, and now that he harassed her this morning, he's definitely not on my list.

Keep your head on, Xander. You don't need to get fired over this idiot. Dr. Sear's warning to me earlier replays in my head.

He turns around and glares at me. I step around him to have my gloves put on me.

The surgery doesn't take too long, and I have to say I'm relieved. The guy sucks the life out of the room, and I wonder again how a girl as sweet as Charlotte could have dated this complete jackass.

The image of him touching her makes my stomach churn, and I have to work extra hard to focus on the patient and not think about him with Charlotte.

After surgery, I have some paperwork to fill out and make my rounds to some patients I've operated on in the last few days. I stop in the lobby and order a few mini blueberry muffins wrapped up to go in case I see Charlotte. Finally in the locker room, I grab my bag and go into the men's shower area. I clean up and get changed into fresh clothes.

When I leave the men's room, Charlotte is backed against the locker, and Damon has her caged with a hand on either side of her face.

"Get away from me, Damon."

"You're a piece of work," Damon seethes at her.

I take a picture on my phone, and a second for good measure, and remind myself I can't hit him or touch him or I'll lose my job. "Step back from her," I angrily tell him as I step right next to him.

Charlotte's head jerks toward me. Damon turns his head but keeps his hands in place. He has a cocky sneer on his face.

A group of four interns come into the locker room, and he takes a step back. "To be continued," he threatens Charlotte and then scowls at me. "You, too."

"What's your deal, man?" I ask him.

He doesn't reply, gives me another look as if he knows something I don't, then picks his bag off the bench and leaves.

"You okay?" I ask Charlotte.

"I'm fine," she mutters and opens her locker, but her hand is shaking.

I put my hand on her back. "Hey."

"I'm fine."

"We should report him. I have a picture of him harassing you."

She shakes her head. "Let it go. He's just mad and hurt."

"Charlotte—"

"Xander, just drop it." She pulls her bag out of her locker and goes into the women's shower area.

There's no way I'm leaving Charlotte here. He could come back, and I'm not taking any chances. I sit down in the lounge area near the door. The TV is on, but I don't hear any of it.

My mind is racing, and I pull up the picture of Damon harassing Charlotte. I want to kill him.

Why is he doing this?

It's a good wait until Charlotte comes out. She's so hot wearing leggings, black boots, and a long-sleeved hot-pink tunic. It's the first time, outside of my dreams, that I've seen her long, blonde hair not pulled up. She's beautiful, and my body hardens. My pulse increases, beating hard in my neck.

She doesn't seem to notice me, goes to her locker and throws her stuff back in it, then grabs her bag and puts her coat on. When she turns to leave, she stops. "Xander. What are you still doing here?"

"Waiting for you."

She shifts on her feet. "You didn't have to wait for me."

"I know I didn't have to. I did it because I wanted to."

She takes a deep breath, and I'm not sure what is going through her mind, but I sense she is grappling with something.

I pull the muffins out of my gym bag. "Plus, I got you these, and you don't want them to go to waste."

A small grin forms on her face. "What is it?"

"Open it."

She cautiously opens the bag then one side of her luscious mouth curves up. "You bought me blueberry muffins?"

"Yep. Are those the ones you love?"

She nods. "Yes. Thank you."

"I also wanted your opinion on surgery number two."

"Surgery number two?"

I adopt a serious expression. "On a scale of one to ten, ten being the worst you've ever experienced, what do you rate the smell when we cut into the patient."

She winces, eye twinkling. "Seven point five."

I tap my chin, considering. "I was thinking seven point eight."

She giggles.

Is this girl for real? She actually laughs at my sick jokes?

I stand up. "Well, I'm ready to get out of here. You done for the day?"

"Yes. I'm all caught up on my paperwork. You want a ride back to your hotel?"

"Sure. If it isn't any trouble?"

She shakes her head. "It's on the way."

"Okay. Thanks." I go to grab her bag.

"What are you doing?"

"I was going to carry your bag for you."

Her eyes widen. "That's nice, but we're at work. Let me carry my own bag."

"Okay."

We walk through the hospital and into the parking garage. When we get in the car, I put my hand on her leg.

She freezes then turns toward me.

"Why is Damon harassing you?"

Charlotte turns to look out the window, as if there's anything interesting in the garage.

"Charlotte, tell me."

Taking a deep breath, she looks back at me. "He says he saw us at Club D. He assumes I cheated on him."

"Nine months ago?"

"Yes."

"But you had already broken up with him."

"I told you that this morning. I'm not a cheater," she snaps.

"I didn't mean to insinuate anything."

"I'm sorry," she says.

"It's okay." I pause, then say, "So he saw us at Club D? In Chicago?"

"Yes."

"And am I to assume we were having a pretty good time?" I wiggle my eyebrows.

She blushes. "You've assumed right." Then she pauses. "Damon saw us leave together, too."

"It's not his business what you do either inside or outside of work. We should report his harassment to HR."

She shakes her head. "No. He's hurt. Let it be. He will stop."

"Charlotte—"

"Xander, can you drop it? Please. I have enough on my mind without dealing with an HR investigation."

Enough on her mind. I'm assuming she means our situation. I squeeze her thigh, realizing my hand is still on it. "Okay. But if he keeps it up, we won't be able to avoid it."

"He won't. It will be fine. I'm sure he was having a bad day and will realize tomorrow he's been a dick and apologize."

I don't expect he'll do that for one minute, but I don't argue. I slowly remove my hand from her thigh.

"Thank you." She starts the car.

We drive for a while. I inhale her flowers-after-the-rain scent and peek at her from time to time. "By the way, you look really nice."

A sexy blush sweeps across her face, and my dick throbs against my zipper.

"Thanks. So do you." Her blue eyes stare into mine briefly then focus back on the road.

"You have plans tonight?"

"Nothing special."

"Wow. So you look this hot when you don't even have plans?" I tease but am not joking. She's smoking hot.

Her blush deepens. "Ha, ha."

I lean closer to her. "I'm serious. You are smoking hot."

"Stop it." She elbows me, but her face lights up.

"So, what do you do when you don't have plans?"

"What do I do?"

"Yes. What are you going to do all night?"

She shrugs. "No clue. What are you going to do all night?"

"I'll go for a run. That's my excitement."

She tightens her grip on the wheel, to all appearances, concentrating on the road.

"Do you want to hang out?" I ask.

She freezes, sitting up straighter.

Crap. I've overstepped the boundaries. But what are the boundaries here? I'm in over my head. I like this girl. I really like her.

But I still have feelings for another woman, and that isn't fair to her.

I'm about to retract my offer when she says, "Okay. What do you want to do?"

Make you cum at least a dozen times and cry out my name all night. Shit, Xander. Stop it.

"I don't know what there is to do here, and especially on a Tuesday night."

She laughs. "What time do you have to be at work tomorrow?"

"Same as today."

"Me, too. Why don't we keep it low-key?"

"I'm good with that." I drum my fingers on my thighs, trying to hide my excitement about spending more time with her. "How do we keep it low-key around here?"

"Why don't you go for your run and come over after. I'll order dinner, and we can play Scrabble."

"Scrabble?"

"Medical term Scrabble." She pulls up to the hotel.

Grinning, I lick my lips. "I'm pretty good at that."

"So, you've said."

"Okay, text me your address when you get home. I'll text you when I'm on my way."

"Deal. But fair disclosure, I'll kick your ass."

"We'll see about that." I lean over and kiss her on the cheek, once again automatically doing it.

She inhales sharply, turns her head toward me, and our lips are inches apart.

I hold myself back from crushing my lips into hers. "I'll see you tonight."

She bites her lip and nods.

"Thanks for the ride." I get out and walk into the hotel as guilt, excitement, and lust all rush through me. I spend the next hour with Billie and Charlotte's faces in my mind, fighting my demons and still not able to remember anything that will put the puzzle pieces of my mind together.

12

Xander

Four Months Earlier

"PIPER AND I NEED TO HEAD BACK TO CHICAGO IN A FEW WEEKS," Noah tells me. We just got done with our run and are both breathing hard and sweating.

We grab bottles of water, and I throw some cash at the vendor. I knew Noah wouldn't stay in New York forever, but I can't say I'm not disappointed.

"Not sure how you can leave New York," I tell him.

"You were going to. You still will." He says with surety and confidence.

"You said I planned to move to Chicago, but there is no way I could ever leave New York."

Noah laughs. "You got your dream position. They are still holding it for you. You'll be moving one of these days. I don't doubt it."

I shake my head, trying to grasp living anywhere besides New York. "Honestly. Can you say you don't miss New York when you're in Chicago?"

Noah shrugs. "Sure. There are things I'll always miss about New York, but Chicago isn't bad. Besides, I got Piper."

I'm happy he has Piper. I like her, too. But a twinge of pain fills my heart that I still haven't found Billie. "Hopefully, I'll find Billie soon, and we can work out whatever happened between us."

Noah stops walking, and sternly says, "Xander, you need to stop this."

"Stop what?"

"Searching for Billie. It's not healthy."

"But I love her."

"No, you don't," he scolds.

"Don't tell me I don't love her."

"You do not love Billie. Stop trying to find her. Why don't you come over and talk to Charlotte and see if you remember her now that you're beginning to remember some things? Maybe then you'll realize you don't love Billie."

I glare at him. "I won't give some poor girl hope I might remember her when I want nothing to do with her."

"You don't know you want nothing to do with her. You've not giving it a chance to see if you remember her."

I grind my teeth. "I would never do that to Billie."

"Jesus, Xander. You're not doing anything to Billie. She's been gone for over ten years. You're way better off without her. When are you going to understand this?"

He's trying to help me, but he doesn't understand. I tell Noah for the hundredth time, "I'll understand it when I either remember it or find Billie."

He sighs, just as frustrated as I am. "You've already started remembering so much. The doctors assume it's only a matter of time before everything comes back enough for you to resume surgery. Come over to my place and visit with Charlotte before she moves back. I'm confident once you spend time with her you'll remember more."

I shake my head. "I already saw her and didn't remember her."

"You were on a ton of meds and had only been awake a few days. Let's try."

I shake my head. "No. It's not fair to use people like that. I'm in love with Billie. I need to find her and work out whatever miscommunication we had. We'll get through it, and then we can be together again."

Noah stares at me like I'm crazy. "She could be married with a dozen kids right now."

She'd better not be.

"If she is, I'll deal with it, but I need to know I at least did all I could to save us."

"Xander—"

"Let's change the subject."

———

A FEW WEEKS PASS, AND NOAH AND PIPER HAVE LEFT FOR CHICAGO. I'm running on my own through Central Park.

"And you wouldn't have any issue moving to Chicago?" A woman with short chestnut hair flashes in my mind. She's sitting behind a big mahogany desk and holding her pen, ready to write all my responses.

"No issues. This is the position I've always wanted. Chicago is a big city, like New York," I tell her.

I stop running as the conversation replays so bright in my mind, it's like it's happening right now.

"Well, Chicago isn't as big as New York," she says.

I laugh. "I'll be okay. In all fairness, I imagine you'll keep me so busy I won't even notice."

She smiles. "You probably are right about that. Do you have a family that needs to relocate?"

"Nope. I'm baggage-free. There's no one to convince or worry about."

"Great. Baggage-free is easier. Makes it a little easier for you to slave away in the operating room all day and night," she jokes.

"I won't have a problem with that, either," I tell her, not to get the job but because it's true. I love being a surgeon.

"The position won't be open for another few months. Dr. Richardson is retiring, and he hasn't given his full resignation date yet, but he's toying with four months."

"I'm fine with that timeline. Like I said, no baggage to worry about."

She writes some notes and puts her pen down. "Dr. Sear and Wemer both gave their approval. The position is yours if you want it."

I stick out my hand. "I definitely want it. Thank you. I'm excited about this."

She shakes my hand. "We are excited to have you on board. As soon as we get further clarification from Dr. Richardson about his retirement date, I'll notify you. How much notice do you need to begin your duties?"

"A two-week notice for my current hospital and long enough for a plane flight."

"That easy, huh?"

"As I said, this is my dream job, and I have no baggage."

I leave the hospital and take an Uber over to Noah's penthouse where I punch in the code and text him I'm there. It doesn't take long before he's next to me, and we are cracking open a celebration beer.

"Thank fuck you got the job. I'm dying here all by myself," Noah says.

"Is it really that bad?"

He sighs. "No, Chicago is fine, I guess. It's a lot harder than I guessed it would be here on my own."

"Haven't you made some friends?"

"No. Only Piper, but she hates me."

I reel back. "Dude, that makes zero sense. She's your friend but hates you?"

"That would be our relationship. Zero sense."

I consider. "So, is this Piper friend slash hater going out with us tonight?"

"I mentioned she hates me, right?"

"So that's a no?"

"Definite no."

I laugh. "I take it you've slept with this girl?"

"Yep. And she's my employee."

My eyes widen. "You didn't dip it in the company ink."

"Oh, but I did. And I knew I shouldn't before, during, and after I did it."

I take a sip of beer and laugh. "Man, Noah. Chicago is doing a number on you, huh?"

"Tell me about it."

"I guess the good news is we both get to hit the town single and free tonight. No baggage to deal with."

Noah gives me a half smile.

I shake my head. "You have it bad for this girl, don't you?"

"I wish I could say no, but I would be lying."

I laugh. "All right. Well, maybe we can change that tonight."

"Please. Put me out of my misery."

"Will do my best. So, where are we going?"

"No idea."

I squint at him. "You've not gone out since you moved, have you?"

"No."

I pull out my phone and scroll for things to do in Chicago. "It's a good thing I'm moving here. You're on track to have the most boring life on earth."

The memory fades, and another portion of my life becomes clear to me. Noah was right. I wanted to move to Chicago and didn't care about leaving New York. I wanted that position.

I stand, stunned for a minute, then run again as the conversation repeats in my mind.

When I get back to my apartment, I pick up my phone, type in Angela Sincroy, and hit the call button.

"Angela Sincroy," she answers.

"Hi, Angela. This is Dr. Xander Kane."

She sounds surprised. "Dr. Kane. How are you feeling?"

"I'm feeling a lot better. Thank you for asking."

"Great to hear."

"Are you still holding the position for me?"

"Yes. Dr. Richardson said he would stay on a few more months if you believe you'll be able to past testing from your doctors by then."

Relieved, I reply, "Yes, I expect I will complete the physical with flying colors."

"That's great, Dr. Kane."

"So, you'll hold the position for me?"

"Yes. As long as you can pass your physicals within the next few months, but I need to tell you Dr. Richardson is getting antsy."

"I understand. Please tell him I appreciate it, and I will be ready."

"That's great to hear. Please have your physicians send all their test reports directly to me."

"Sounds good, Angela. Thank you."

"Great to speak with you, Dr. Kane. I'm glad you're recovering."

"Me, too. Thank you. I'll talk to you soon." I disconnect and sit back, looking out into the New York skyline. There are no more doubts. My life is waiting for me in Chicago.

Charlotte

Present Day

MY STOMACH HAS BEEN IN KNOTS ALL EVENING.

Why did I agree to hang out with Xander?

Because you've never wanted anyone as much as you want him.

You're in way over your head.

My attraction toward Xander has only gotten stronger throughout the day. I'm so comfortable around him, and every time he looks at me or touches me, I get a rush of endorphins.

I gaze over at the brown bag I put on my counter, pull out a blueberry muffin, and eat it. The sweet things he did for me today, like buying me this treat, trying to carry my bag, and kissing me on the cheek race around my mind, never mind how he waited for me to make sure I was okay in the locker room after the Damon incident.

Damon. He was so angry today. I pull out my phone and text him.

"I know what you believe, but I've never lied to you, and I'm not lying now. We were over when I met him."

"You're such a whore," comes flying back, and my gut flips.

"Stop this. You're better than this. I realize you're hurt, but this isn't the way to act. I would never have cheated on you."

"Doesn't even matter. Even if you got with him after we broke up, within a week, you were with someone else. WHORE."

I stare at the screen in shock. I shouldn't be surprised at Damon's cruelty after the last encounter I had with him.

"I'm sorry you feel that way. From now on, don't talk to me or touch me." There. At least I have a written trail if I need it for any reason.

Better not tell Xander about this. He will flip and have me in HR first thing tomorrow.

Xander. My pulse creeps up, thinking about him. And I need to stop it. I remind myself he still has feelings for Billie, and he may never lose them.

I panic and consider canceling on him but can't seem to do it. So instead, I tell myself I'll only be friends with him. That's what he needs right now anyways—friends who care about him and can help him.

Keep it in the friendship zone, I tell myself, right as the door buzzes. I push the button, and his voice comes through the speaker.

It doesn't take long before he's knocking on my door. I open it, and he has on the black wool cap he looks super-hot in. He steps inside, he bends down, and kisses me on the cheek.

I freeze for the third time today.

"Sorry. I don't know why I keep doing that," he says.

"It's okay. Come in. Here, let me take your coat."

He steps farther inside and removes his jacket. He's wearing a long-sleeved knit top that hugs his body perfectly and a pair of designer jeans. My heart beats a little faster.

Why does he have to look so good?

He hands me his coat, and I put it in my closet. When I turn around, he's standing still with a strange expression on his face.

"Xander?"

His face is pale.

"What's wrong?"

He shakes his head. "I feel like I've been here before."

A chill moves through me, and I softly reply, "You have."

"No, this is different. Give me a minute if you don't mind?"

"Take all the time you need."

Glancing around the room, he focuses on my kitchen, plods over and sits down on a barstool. His face scrunches up, and he gazes from side to side.

I approach, and he pulls out the chair next to him. "Can you sit here for a minute?"

Excitement passes through me then a caution sign blinks in my mind.

Does he remember?

Don't get too excited.

A few minutes pass before he murmurs, "Will you humor me?"

"Sure."

"Can you stand up?"

I do. He grasps me around the waist and pulls me onto his lap. I take a deep breath, and he draws me closer.

"Will you put your arm around me."

My heart is beating so loud, I'm sure he can hear it. His sexy scent is filling every cell of my body. "Put my arm around you?"

His eyes are wide, lips twitching a little. "Please?"

I know what his brain is trying to remember, and I put my arm around him exactly the way I did that day: around his shoulders, slightly bent, running my fingers through his hair. But he has his cap on, so I'm stroking him on top of it. "Like this?" I murmur.

He removes his hat. His face is inches from mine, and his lips are so close. "Do it now?"

I run my fingers through his hair the same way I did that day.

His right arm moves slowly from the counter to my body then back again. "That's not right," he mutters.

I stop.

"No, keep doing what you're doing but get closer." His left arm pulls me in, and I lean into him as close as I did that day, feeling his heart beat against his chest.

I exhale and stroke his hair again.

His right arm moves from the counter to my mouth then he repeats it several times, and his eyes widen. He stops moving. I stop moving.

Slowly, Xander looks at me. "Did I feed you pancakes?"

"Yes," I whisper.

"And you wore a black silk robe?"

Tears well up, and I blink repeatedly, willing myself not to cry. "Yes."

He remembers me?

Xander pushes his forehead to mine. "Then I did this."

A tear falls down my cheek, and he wipes it away with his thumb, pauses, then says, "And then I did this." He weaves his fingers through my hair until he grasps it by the roots, and he softly parts my lips with his tongue, moving me so I'm straddling him. He embraces me, both hands cupping my head, so I can't go anywhere.

The heaven I learned only with Xander is upon me, and I fall back into it, not considering anything except him and how my body is buzzing in his arms.

My feet plant themselves on the footrest of the barstool, and my lower body automatically grinds against his growing erection.

We are both breathing hard, and his lips move across my jawline, to my earlobe, down my neck then back to my mouth.

Claiming me.

Worshiping me.

Making me feel like nothing has happened in the last six months, and he only wants me—like no other woman exists or ever could, going forward.

The doorbell rings, and I barely hear it. It rings again. "I think someone is here," Xander mumbles against my lips.

I pull back. "What?"

The bell rings again. My face flushes. "Oh, the food. Let me find my purse." I jump off his lap, confused about what this means.

Does he remember everything now? Does he still have feelings for Billie?

"I got it." Xander goes to the door and buzzes the delivery guy in. He steps into the hallway for him to arrive.

I try to pull myself together, still breathless and telling myself not to freak out.

Xander comes back in the kitchen with food, and I open one of the cabinets, but I stare, not sure what I'm trying to accomplish.

I must have stood there too long because Xander comes behind me and wraps his arms around me. "Hey, you're shaking."

I close my eyes, wanting to stay forever in his embrace, but I take a deep breath. "I'm fine."

"Charlotte." He turns me to face him. "I'm sorry if I made you uncomfortable."

He thinks he made me uncomfortable? "You didn't."

He scans my eyes. "No?"

"No." I tell myself not to ask him, but my mouth betrays me. "What else about me do you remember?"

Xander takes a deep breath. "That's the only thing I remember, besides my dreams."

"And do you remember anything else...about your twenties?" I almost say her name, but I don't.

His face falls, and he shakes his head.

My gut drops, and I blink away tears once more.

Xander cups my face. "I'm sorry."

"You have nothing to be sorry about." I let out a shaky breath.

Xander's thumb circles on my cheek. "Maybe things will come back now. This memory has to be good, right?"

He's right. But it hurts that he still has feelings for another woman. I'm so over my head, and I blurt out, "I don't know what I'm doing anymore."

Xander's jaw tenses. "Do you want me to stay away from you?"

I reach for him, pull him into my body, and blurt out, "No!"

He hardens against my stomach as my pulse increases and my sex throbs. Heat fills his eyes. I throw all my worries and thoughts away about how he has feelings for anyone else besides me and succumb to the moment.

"Charlotte—"

I put my finger over his mouth and stare at him.

He kisses my finger while his eyes never leave mine.

Suddenly, he bends down, picks me up, his lips moving over mine. I wrap my legs around his body and he carries me into the bedroom. I pull his shirt over his head, and he grabs my tunic and pulls it off me before slipping his fingers into my leggings and gliding them into my already drenched sex.

I moan.

"I love your sounds," he whispers in my ear, nibbling at my lobe, circling my clit with his thumb while curling his finger in my heat.

"Oh God," I breath. "I've missed you so much."

"I've missed you. Every night you remind me how much," he murmurs, nuzzling my breasts. His free hand glides under my back and quickly unlatches my bra, as his other fingers continue to drive me to my high.

Whimpering, I grasp his head, pushing his mouth harder onto my breasts.

Warmth moves through me as his tongue slides across my nipples, his fingers circle my pussy, and his hard body lies against mine.

My chest is heaving, trying to find air.

"Xander," I cry out, as his eyes drill into mine and his fingers push me over the edge, shattering me to pieces. He consumes my mouth with his, continuing to finger fuck me through my high.

I'm clutching him, and he rolls me over on top of him, kissing me with so much heat I don't know if I'm dizzy from my orgasm or his kisses.

"Please tell me you have condoms," he murmurs.

"In the drawer."

He fumbles with my drawer and yanks out a strip of condoms, ripping one open while it's still attached to the strip.

I unbuckle his pants, and work them off him, then remove my leggings, quickly crawling back into his arms.

Nothing on earth has ever made me feel as safe or wanted as I'm in his arms.

"Hold me tighter," I whisper, and he draws me closer to him, making me forget any imperfection could ever exist in our relationship.

I sink onto him, moaning.

"So much better than my dreams," he whispers, leaving no question in my mind how much he wants or needs me, as we writhe in a fury of desire.

I hold on to him tighter than I've ever held anyone. Maybe it's because I'm scared that once this is over, he'll be gone. Perhaps it's because it's been so long since I've been able to hold him. Maybe it's because I assumed I had lost him completely. Whatever the reason, we're both clinging to each other so tight, only our hips can thrust.

We never stop kissing. Except for words or moans coming out of our mouths, our lips and tongues never move away.

And I'm lost in all that is Xander. All we were before the accident. All we've gone through the last six months. All we are right at this moment.

As confusing as this situation may be, the one thing that doesn't faze me is my desire to be his.

And I want to be his only.

Xander

I'M LOST IN EVERYTHING THAT IS CHARLOTTE. HER BLUE EYES, THE soft sea of blonde hair, and her flushed cheeks I'm holding in my hands consume me. A never-ending flame burns into all my cells as her mouth and tongue caress mine.

The scent of flowers after the rain is stronger than in my dreams, and when I hear her moan or cry out my name, it's as if I'm somehow home.

That's how Charlotte makes me feel...like home.

Billie never made you feel this way.

The thought lodges in my brain, but I push past it, not wanting to miss a single moment of having Charlotte in my arms.

Night after night, I dreamed of her. Faceless for six months, then last night, it was even more real when I saw her face, but tonight, right now, it's the most intense moment I've ever had.

"You're perfect," I tell her as I stare into her blue eyes. And she is. Every single part of her. "We're perfect together," I say to her, not able to control what comes out of my mouth.

I don't know what it is, but around her, I say whatever is on my mind, without holding back or wondering if I should say it or not.

Her eyes catch mine, and her head nods. The most gorgeous mouth I've ever seen is in the O that has been haunting my dreams every night.

She slightly shudders, like in my dream, but this time, it's real. She's here, in my arms. I pull her even tighter into me before my hands drop from her back and cup her ass, as her walls spasm.

"Xander," she whimpers, digging her fingers into my shoulders as her breasts heave against my chest.

I taste the salt of her skin, more prominent than in my dreams, and I taste it again, sucking on the curve of her neck, licking her collarbone, elated by every noise that comes out of her glorious mouth.

Her skin is like glitter, shining in the dark. Warm and smooth, it slides against my flesh, melting into me.

"Beautiful. You're so fucking beautiful," I tell her as she vibrates harder, and her eyes blink, trying to focus.

How can she be so perfect?

"Xander," she whimpers, and my balls tighten.

I thrust into her harder. "I...I...oh...," she cries out as her walls collapse against my cock and send me into a wonderland of adrenaline.

Gripping her harder, I pump into her forcefully, as she oscillates on top of me in the most beautiful, angelic eruption I've ever seen.

I keep my arms wrapped around her, stroking her lower back and ass, entwining my legs with hers as she nuzzles my neck. Breathing hard, I don't move, wanting to keep her right where she is forever. I'm not sure how many times I kiss the top of her head.

I don't know what she's pondering, but I'm full of emotions and, if I open my mouth, I can't guarantee what will come out. So I stroke her head and continue to shower her with kisses, holding her tight.

The memory of feeding her pancakes while she wore a black silk robe, and screwing on her barstool, flies back to me. It was probably four in the morning, and her stomach growled. She admitted she hadn't eaten that day, and I cooked for her.

"We need pancakes," I said to her.

"Pancakes?" She looked at me funny.

I grinned at her. "Yeah, pancakes. You stay in bed, and I'll make them."

"You want to make me pancakes?" She looked at me like she didn't believe me.

I laughed and kissed her then got up, threw a towel around my waist, and headed for the kitchen. She came out in her robe and watched me. When they were ready, I sat down on the barstool and pulled her into my lap then fed her, which then led to sex right where we sat.

The memory is crystal clear, and hope grows inside me that the rest of the holes in my mind will eventually be filled.

Charlotte slowly moves her head out of my neck and looks up at me. I peck her lips. Stroking her cheek, I stare into her eyes. "You okay?"

She smiles and nods. "What are you thinking about?"

"Pancakes."

She laughs. "You must really like pancakes."

I grin at her. "I do."

She laughs.

God, her laugh is sexy and sweet.

"It's so vivid. It gives me hope."

She cups my face. "Never lose hope, Xander."

I know hope is important to her. There was a text conversation about her days in the orphanage and hope. It's another reminder to me about how special she is. And it makes me want to protect her against the world and anyone who tries to harm her.

"Don't lose hope in me," I whisper to her and blink as emotion overcomes me.

I'm a man who can't remember over a decade of important pieces of his life. And it plays with my mind, making me question who I am and what kind of person. And I think about Charlotte and all she's already gone through, and then I think about what I've put her through and still am, and my soul gets crushed. I struggle with hatred toward myself for hurting her, my inability to remember my own life, and my thoughts and feelings for an ex-flame I'm told I shouldn't think twice about, when the most beautiful woman on earth is right in front of me.

"Shh." She puts her finger to my lips. "I won't. I promise."

I blink. A tear falls down my cheek, and I turn away from her, ashamed of my inability to have my life together.

She kisses my tear away, and her luscious lips are on mine, pulling me back into the Nirvana that only exists with her.

"Stay the night," she whispers.

"Yeah? I can?"

"Yeah." She reclaims my lips as hers, and I realize how alone and empty I've felt these last few months, like a piece of my soul has been missing.

Charlotte makes me feel whole again. As messed up as my head is, she still wants me and is putting up with shit she shouldn't have to deal with. But she is.

I cup her face and pull back from her kiss. "Hey."

She scans my eyes.

"I have a Scrabble game to beat you at."

She laughs.

"You have some blankets?"

She tilts her head at me. "Yes. Why?"

"I'll play in my boxers. Clothing is optional for you, but I'm biased toward your black silk robe." I wink at her.

Charlotte arches a brow. "Is this your way of trying to distract me?"

"It's my way of trying to keep you half naked all night, but I won't have a problem undressing you again when the time comes."

"Is that all talk or a promise?"

I lick my lips and say, "That's a promise."

———

WEARING HARDLY ANY CLOTHES AND WRAPPED UP IN BLANKETS, WE eat cold Chinese food and play Scrabble for hours, creating medical words any average person would find disgusting or not even know is a word.

We're on our third game, which is the tiebreaker, and Charlotte creates a word worth 167 points.

"You have to be kidding me," I groan.

She throws her arm in the air. "I win!"

"You're the master of gore," I tell her.

She beams.

I laugh. "That's pretty hot."

"That's what you told me the first night you met me."

I stare at her in question, wishing I could remember meeting her but having no recollection.

"I grossed Vivian and Quinn out when I told you I liked pus more than blood because it's less predictable."

"That is hot."

She smiles at me, lighting up the room, and I wonder how she became the amazing person she is when she had gone through so much as a child.

How could no one have ever loved her, yet she's still so sweet and kind and loving?

I must stare at her too long because she nervously asks, "What?"

I crawl over and pull her into my lap. "Tell me about what it was like to grow up in an orphanage."

She freezes, staring at me, not breathing.

"Sorry. I swear my brain doesn't work correctly around you. You don't have to answer that."

Charlotte lets out a breath. "It's lonely and sad."

I stroke her hair and pull her closer. "How old were you when you got there?"

"Three."

My heart is breaking, and I don't know why I'm making her tell me this. I can tell it's painful, but I continue asking her questions.

"What happened?"

"My parents died in a crash, and there wasn't anyone to take me."

"I'm sorry."

She swallows hard then shrugs.

I imagine a blonde-haired, blue-eyed, three-year-old, scared, sad, and lonely. My heart bleeds more for her.

Stroking her cheek, I tell her, "I think you're amazing."

She gives me a sad smile, then says, "What about your parents? They were traveling when you had your accident?"

"They're retired and aren't in the country often. I've seen them a few times since then, but they are somewhere in Europe right now. I lose track where."

"I already know you don't have any siblings..."

"No, there's just me."

"So who's been watching you since the accident?"

I laugh. "No one. I can take care of myself."

She tilts her head at me and scans my eyes. "That sounds lonely."

My pulse goes up. The guys have been there for me, but it has been lonely...and depressing, too.

Her hands lace together behind my head, and I get this strange sense of déjà vu, but I can't pinpoint it. "I can't imagine how hard this has been on you. I'm here if you ever need to talk, Xander."

A wave of emotion hits me so hard I have to blink tears back, and I turn my head away from her.

"Hey," she softly says, and I turn back to her. Her hand brushes the side of my head. "Everything will be okay."

How does she know?

It's as if she's tapping into my thoughts, digging into the fear I have that things are never truly going to be okay again. It's a simple phrase, "everything will be okay," and I've heard it from many people. Somehow, coming from Charlotte, it's like she actually understands my fears without me even saying them.

It's like everything from the last six months comes rushing to the surface, and the dam breaks. Maybe it's because I held it in for so long, or possibly because she is the only one who seems to understand me, but she pulls me into her chest, and I have a total breakdown, as tears flow out of me.

Charlotte holds me tight, kissing the top of my head.

"What if it never comes back," I choke out.

"Everything will still be okay.

"Will it?"

"Yes." She says it as if there is no room to argue, and it makes me believe, if only at that moment, it will be.

She pulls away and cups my cheeks in her hands. Her blue eyes, full of compassion, stare into mine. "What's the worst part of not remembering?"

"Originally the frustration or confusion of not remembering, but that's no longer the worst thing."

"What is?"

I haven't known her for years, and besides my dreams, reading old text messages, and the pancakes, I don't remember our time together. Technically, I've only been around her for a few days, but everything about Charlotte makes me feel like I've known her forever, and she's special. And I know her last six months have been painful because of me. "That I've hurt you."

She blinks back her tears and uses her thumbs to wipe away the tears seeping out of my eyes. She says, "That's not your fault."

"It is."

"No, it's not."

"I hate myself for it." And I do. I'm not only telling her that. In the last two days, I've beaten myself up too many times to count over the fact I've caused her any pain in her life. She's already had a lifetime's worth and deserves nothing but to be loved.

She puts her forehead to mine. "Don't."

I turn from her. She lays her palm on my cheek and brings me back to face her. "Don't."

How can she not hate me for what I've put her through?

A different confusion fills my mind as I melt into her blue eyes full of concern for me, when I deserve anything but that from her.

Then she kisses me, giving herself once again so freely to me, telling me she will be mine forever if I want her.

It kills me further, as I kiss her back, not able to control myself, but knowing I need to get my memory back and get Billie out of my head once and for all. I'm not 100 percent Charlotte's until I do. And that's what she deserves.

We make love several times throughout the night. When I finally fall asleep, Charlotte is curled in my arms, and everything feels right. I have a notion things will be okay, that going forward, I won't hurt her anymore, but that is my mistake.

I should have stayed awake.

Xander

"Yes, Billie, don't stop," I tell her as she circles her hips on my cock.

"You like that?" She stops.

"Don't be a tease." I grasp her hips and move them myself.

She giggles, and her honey-colored hair falls against my face as she leans down and kisses me.

I pull her into me, groaning as she moves again.

"Faster, Billie," I beg.

She moves faster, and my balls tighten.

"Oh, I'm so close," I tell her.

She slows down. "Don't you want to be with me more?"

"Of course I want to be with you more."

"Good. Quit talking." She speeds up then, out of nowhere, slows again.

"Fuuuuuuck, Billie," I yell out.

"Come on, Xander," she coos. "Quit, and I'll give you more of this." She circles her hips again.

"Yes. Do that."

She stops. "If you want it, you'll quit."

Is she seriously withholding sex?

I push her off me, even though my dick wants to explode.

She narrows her eyes. "You don't love me."

"You know I love you, Billie."

She glares at me. "If you loved me, you'd let my parents pay for your school, and you'd quit your paramedic job."

I scoff. "If you loved me, you wouldn't ask me to do something like that."

"We never spend time together anymore. You're making this choice."

"Everything I'm doing is so we can have a good life. It's all for our future."

"You don't need to be a paramedic anymore. Let my parents pay and go to school. We can see each other more."

"No. I don't accept handouts, and you know it."

"Xander, I will not waste my twenties waiting for you."

I jerk my head at her. "Waiting for me?"

"Yes. Sitting on the sidelines and only seeing you every so often."

"What exactly are you saying? Why don't you be crystal clear so I don't misinterpret this." I glare at her.

She softly replies, "You don't love me anymore, do you?"

I roll my eyes. She's just being dramatic. I pull her into me. "Of course I love you. I've only ever loved you, Billie."

"Then quit."

"I won't do that, and you know it."

She pokes my chest with a finger. "Quit, or we're done."

"Done?"

"Yes."

"Let me get this straight. I either quit my job and let your parents pay for my med school, or we break up. No more Billie and Xander. Do I understand this correctly?"

She blinks back tears, puts her hands on her hips, and says, "Yes. Make up your mind because I'm tired of waiting."

I take a deep breath. So this is what it's come to? I step forward, wrap her in my arms, and kiss her then pull back. "I'm not quitting, so tell me you are not thinking correctly and are just emotional. I love you, Billie, and you love me. Tell me you are just venting right now."

She shakes her head. "I am not emotional. I am not venting. I am thinking correctly. Quit, or we're done."

I jerk my head back in shock and shake my head. "No."

Sadness fills her eyes. "I hope you get everything you want in life, Xander."

"Billie." I clasp her hand and try to pull her to me, but she yanks away. After throwing on her clothes, she walks to the door.

"Billie, you're the only person I'll ever love, and you know that. Don't do this."

With tears swimming in her eyes, she gives me a final look. "Goodbye, Xander."

And then she's gone. "Fuck!" I plop down and punch the pillow on the sofa, in shock for a moment, wondering if we are really done.

Out of nowhere, music plays. It gets louder and louder and finally is so loud, it snaps me back into reality. I sit up in bed, reach for my phone on the nightstand, and turn off the alarm. It takes me a few seconds to register I'm not in my New York apartment. Where am I?

I turn toward the window. Charlotte, sitting in an armchair, her knees curled into her chest, with her lip shaking and tears streaming down her face.

Oh God. What the hell did I just do?

I jump off the bed to go to her, but before I can get around the bed, she says, "Xander, you need to go."

"Charlotte, I—"

She cuts me off, and more tears stream down her face. "Please, just go."

"Charlotte—"

"Please, go," she cries out. "I can't do this. I thought I could, but I can't. You're in love with someone else. Please go."

"But—"

"Please. If you care about me at all, you'll go." Tears are falling fast out of her eyes, and my heart breaks.

What did I say in my sleep? I wince.

"Please, just go," she whispers.

I throw on my clothes and glance at her one last time. She points to the door, and I turn and leave.

It's around three in the morning, and the cold darkness embraces me like a blanket, a stark contrast to the warmth and light Charlotte represents.

My hotel is several miles away, and I run as I beat myself up, over and over.

I hurt her. Again.

The dream replays in my mind. I hadn't believed Noah when he told me Billie wanted me to quit and let her parents pay for my school. Now I do. I know it's what happened.

But what did I say while I was sleeping?

I cringe, thinking about what I might have said, and how she could have taken it.

Fuck.

I should have stayed away from Charlotte. Until I learned the truth about Billie and me, I should have stayed away. My mind isn't to be trusted right now.

But I never dreamed about anyone except Charlotte. Why did I have to dream about Billie when I was with Charlotte?

I curse myself, a million times, hating myself for the pain Charlotte has endured because of me.

When I arrive at my hotel, I'm full of self-loathing, sadness, and anger. My heart is beating hard, but I feel like it's been ripped open.

I shower, sling my bag over my shoulder, and leave for work. I'm early, but I can't stay in the hotel room because I need to pull it together.

The Uber pulls up, and I get in, wishing I was sitting next to Charlotte in her car. I put the palms of my hands against my eyes and try to figure out a strategy on how to not make her hurt any worse today when I'm around her.

When I get in the lobby, I have four mini blueberry muffins wrapped up, and I buy a coffee with cream and two sugars and put a stopper in it so it stays hot. I go to the locker room and open Charlotte's locker with the code I saw her use the day before.

I set the coffee and bag in it, then lock it, and go to my locker.

It's best if I'm not here when Charlotte comes in.

After I get ready, I read the schedule. I have two surgeries without Charlotte and the third one with her.

And just because the universe has to play cruel jokes on me, my first two surgeries are with Damon.

Awesome. I take a few deep breaths and remind myself I need to keep it cool where he's concerned. The last thing I want is to lose my job and be back in New York.

I never thought I would want to live anywhere but New York, but now that I know Charlotte and that she's here, there is no way I'm leaving Chicago unless she's with me.

My perspective has shifted.

My reality is no longer the past.

My truth is no longer the same.

It hits me hard. Billie is my past. I haven't loved her for a long time. While I did love her when we broke up, I don't remember falling out of love with her. But I no longer care.

Charlotte is my future. She is who I love. Whatever I have to do to make her mine, and win her back, I will.

I pray she will give me another chance.

16

Charlotte

HE WAS HAVING SEX WITH BILLIE. IN MY BED.

I try to push it out of my mind, but I can't.

"Yes, Billie, don't stop."

"Faster, Billie."

"Fuuuuuuck, Billie."

"You know I love you, Billie."

"Of course I love you. I've only ever loved you, Billie."

"Billie, you're the only person I'll ever love, and you know that."

Xander's words recycle in my mind like a cyclone, spinning over and over, ripping through my heart.

What was I thinking? I knew he still had feelings for her. Playing with fire, that's what I was doing, and I knew it. I allowed myself to pretend it was okay. That Xander would realize that was then, and this is now, and love me again.

But he still loves her.

He doesn't remember loving me. Pancakes and dreams of fucking me are all he remembers. Text messages reveal our past, but that doesn't help him remember he loved me.

And he did. He told me he did. And then everything changed.

"You should come to New York and surprise me," he texted me the night before I did exactly that.

We had only met twice. One night at Club D, once in Columbus. He fed me pancakes, and we screwed so many times in those two short encounters ,I lost track.

After that, we spent a few months communicating every way possible; texting, talking on the phone, emailing, Facetiming each other.

Every single day we communicated any chance we got.

When Piper was in New York and asked if I wanted to bid on him in a charity date auction, I didn't think twice and was willing to drop up to ten grand to make sure no other woman won. Piper had an old lady bid secretly on him, and she sent me a photo of the paddle. I texted him the picture with a heart drawn around it and, "I own you."

When he suggested I fly out and surprise him on his day off, I didn't think twice. He had to stay in New York to pack for his new job in Chicago. Within two hours, I'd hopped on a red-eye, and the taxi dropped me off at his building at five in the morning.

I rang the buzzer.

"Hello."

"I'm here to collect my property," I teased.

He didn't even respond but ran down twelve flights of stairs, he told me later. He opened the door and wrapped his arms around me, picking me up and kissing me with so much intensity, I was breathless.

"Are you really here?" Xander asked when we paused for breath.

I kissed him more.

He cupped my face. "You're officially the coolest girl ever."

"You owe me a date, but I want my dessert first," I teased him.

He picked me up over his shoulder, carried me into the elevator, and, once we got into his apartment, we didn't leave the bedroom until after noon.

His apartment had boxes all over it, but he unpacked a box to dress up so he could take me to a fancy dinner I remember little of because we were lip-locked the entire meal.

I had to be back in Chicago the next day for work. I had gotten out of the morning surgeries but couldn't get out of the one at four o'clock in the afternoon.

Xander insisted on driving me to the airport for my flight at seven in the morning. We were almost to the airport, on the expressway, when Xander clasped my hand, looked at me, and said, "Don't forget I love you, Charlotte."

I smiled bigger than I ever had before. "Don't forget I love you, too," I said right as a driver entering the highway smashed into us, and the car spun in circles.

After that, everything was bloody, full of glass, and red flashing lights.

When I finally saw him, he looked me in the eyes and told me he was sorry but didn't remember me and then asked Noah about Billie.

For six months I tried coming to terms with the fact I needed to move on because he was in love with someone else, not me.

Then he came back into my life and reminded me over and over why I love him so much.

But nothing has changed. He still loves Billie, and now he's dreaming about her, not me.

I step out of the hot shower and towel off.

Get your shit together, Charlotte.

I stare at my puffy eyes in the mirror and try to apply makeup but give up. What is the point?

I get dressed for work, repack my bag, and head out.

As I drive to work, I try to figure out how to deal with Xander.

Keep it professional. Only look and talk to him if you have to during surgery. Do not put yourself in a situation to be alone with him.

I park my car, walk into the hospital, and make my way to the locker room, avoiding all conversations with anyone I can. When I step into the room, I read the schedule first.

No surgeries with Xander until later this afternoon. *Thank you, universe.* At least I'll have a few hours to continue pulling it together.

I go to my locker and unlock it to find a coffee, along with a brown bag. I close my eyes for a moment. Xander.

"Wow, you have a secret admirer or something? I'd die to have a coffee waiting for me." Tabi's voice rings in my ear.

I open my eyes. She's staring at me.

"Hey, you okay?"

"Yes. I didn't sleep well last night, that's all."

She tilts her head. "Please tell me Damon didn't leave that for you?"

I shake my head hard. "No. He doesn't know my code. Plus, I'm sure he hates me right now."

"Why?"

I shrug. I'm definitely not telling Tabi anything about Damon and me.

"Who knows your code, if it isn't him?"

"No one. Forget you saw it," I tell her.

Tabi reaches in and puts her hands around the coffee. "It's still hot. You'd better drink it, especially if you didn't get any sleep."

I realize the only way to not have Tabi ask any more questions is to take the coffee and drink it. I pull out the stopper and take a sip.

She picks up the bag and opens up. "Blueberry muffins. Yum."

"You can have one," I tell her.

She reaches in, retrieves one, and hands it to me then she snatches one for herself. "To your secret admirer!" She grins and taps her muffin to mine.

When we're done eating, she announces, "Well, I have surgery with the devil himself this morning. At least you don't have to deal with that on no sleep!"

She doesn't seem to have any love for Damon anymore. Not that I can blame her.

"At least I can ogle the new eye candy. Have you noticed how hot Dr. Kane is?"

My face flushes, but I shrug my shoulders. "He's okay," I lie to her.

"Okay? Have you not looked at that boy?"

I try to blow her off. "Just another doctor. Okay, I have to get moving here. I'll see you later, Tabi."

"Wish me luck." She rolls her eyes.

"Best of luck. See you later."

I shut my locker door and take my coffee with me, almost to my surgery room when I run into Xander.

My heart beats faster, and I can tell from the emotion in his eyes he feels terrible, but he doesn't bring it up.

"Morning," he says with a little smile.

"Hey." I can't help the small smile forming on my face.

We say nothing, just stare at each other. It isn't uncomfortable, which makes it hurt more because, from the moment I met Xander, everything was always so comfortable between us.

I hold up my coffee. "Thanks."

He smiles bigger. "Still hot?"

I nod.

"Good." He scans my eyes again. "Well, I get to spend the next six hours listening to the fifties channel, so wish me luck."

I bite my lip and smile. "Have fun with that."

He raises his eyebrows at me. "I'll see you in surgery later."

"Okay."

Xander opens the door to his operating room. Damon is there, and I feel bad that Xander has to deal with him all morning. Damon's eyes catch mine and then glance at Xander, and I have no doubt he'll be an ass all day.

I get through my two surgeries and have a few hours to kill, so I retrieve my laptop from my locker and sit in the lounge area of the locker room to get some work done. I turn off the TV and am engrossed in my reports when a low voice mutters, "Whore."

My insides quiver. I don't need to look to see who it is. Sure enough, I turn my head to see Damon sauntering past me.

Taking a deep breath, I say nothing to him and return to reading my reports, hoping he will leave me alone.

Luck is not on my side today.

"Filthy whore," he asserts from his locker, which is at least one hundred feet away.

We are the only people in the room. I am debating what to do when he comes over and drops a pair of black lace panties in front of me. "Thought you would want these back, although maybe you don't even wear panties anymore since you're such a whore."

Damon is taking things to an outrageous level. He saunters back to his locker, and I shove my laptop in my bag then bolt out of the room, eyes on the floor, and run right into a rock-hard chest.

"Charlotte, you're shaking. What's wrong?" Xander pulls my chin up and gazes into my eyes.

"Charlotte, what happened?" Dr. Wemer is standing next to him.

"Nothing." I try to walk past them, but Xander holds my shoulders.

"Is he in there?" Xander's eyes blaze.

"He?" Dr. Wemer asks.

"Damon," Xander grits out.

"Charlotte, tell me what is going on," Dr. Wemer sternly demands.

Xander tries to move me aside, but I dig in my heels. "Don't. You'll get fired," I tell him.

Dr. Wemer moves to block the door.

"Move," Xander barks at him.

Dr. Wemer braces himself in the doorway. "Not the way to handle this. You two, come with me."

"Get out of the way," Xander seethes.

"No. Turn around right now and come with me," Dr. Wemer instructs.

"Xander." I cup his face, so he has to look at me.

His eyes are full of rage.

"Please. Don't," I beg him again.

He takes a deep breath. "Okay. But this ends now. You're reporting all of this."

"All right. Come with me." I reach for his hand.

Xander sags. "Okay."

Dr. Wemer pats him on the shoulder. "Good choice."

"There better be consequences."

Dr. Wemer starts down the hallway. "There will be. Let's go."

As we follow, I release Xander's hand and fix my gaze ahead.

I assume we are going to HR, but Dr. Wemer takes us to Dr. Sear's office.

Dr. Wemer knocks on the door. "Can we come in?"

Dr. Sear points to the table in his office. "Have a seat. What's going on?" He closes his laptop. "Charlotte, you okay?"

I settle on the edge of a chair as Dr. Wemer says, "There's been an incident."

"Tell me you didn't do something stupid," Dr. Sear asks, his steely gaze on Xander who is sitting as well, as rigid as if a touch would shatter him into a thousand pieces.

"No, he didn't," Dr. Wemer asserts.

"Good. Tell me what happened."

"Charlotte, go ahead," Dr. Wemer orders.

Heat creeps up my neck. I'm not sure where to begin.

Xander scowls "I don't know what happened today, but Damon has been harassing Charlotte. He's upset she broke up with him."

Dr. Sear cocks his head. "Charlotte, is this true?"

"Y-yes."

"What is your role in this, Xander?" Dr. Sear asks Xander.

Xander doesn't flinch. "I met Charlotte the weekend I came to interview for this position. She had broken up with him already, but he saw us together at a club."

"You two knew each other?"

"Charlotte was visiting me in New York when we got into the accident that broke her foot and where I lost my memory."

"He doesn't remember me, and I didn't know he was even in Chicago, so I didn't know what to say when you introduced us the other day." I try to keep emotion out of my voice and state the facts.

Dr. Sear and Dr. Wemer do their best not to appear shocked, but it's clear they are.

"So, you two are dating?" Dr. Wemer asks.

"No," I say, just as Xander states, "Yes."

Xander's jaw clenches, and he tips his face up, eyes blinking fast.

The room is so quiet you can hear a pin drop. It seems like forever, but Dr. Sear finally asks, "Charlotte, what happened today?"

This is so embarrassing. "I was working on my laptop in the lounge area of the locker room, and Damon came in and called me a whore. After I ignored him, he threw a pair of my underwear I must have left at his house at me. He told me he thought I would want them back, but maybe I didn't wear them anymore because I'm such a whore."

Xander bolts off his chair and almost gets to the door, but Dr. Wemer cuts him off. "Go sit down."

"Move," he demands.

"Xander, sit your ass down now!" Dr. Sear hurls at him.

Xander's shoulders flex, and he reluctantly returns to sit next to me.

"What happened when I was in the locker room?" Dr. Sear asks.

"He accused me of 'playing in the sandbox' when I came into the locker room with Xander."

Xander pulls out his phone and shows Dr. Sear a picture. "This happened yesterday afternoon."

"What happened then?" Dr. Sear asks.

"He called me a whore and accused me of cheating on him with Xander. But I didn't," I add, a little too quickly.

"No one is accusing you of anything, nor would it matter," Dr. Sear assures.

"Why didn't you two report this yesterday?" Dr. Wemer asks.

"Charlotte didn't want to. She thought he would stop," Xander grits out.

"I texted him last night, thinking he was just hurt and would stop, but it didn't help."

Xander's head snaps toward me. "You texted him last night."

I give a slow nod.

An expression I can't understand crosses Xander's face.

"Let me see the messages." Dr. Sear holds out his hand.

I pull out my phone, bring up the text chain, and hand it to him. He scans it then passes it to Dr. Wemer. After Dr. Wemer reads it, he holds it out to me, but Xander snatches it.

Great. Add more fuel to the fire.

"Piece of shit," Xander mumbles, then returns it to me.

"Is there anything else you want to disclose?" Dr. Sear asks.

"No."

"We need to disclose this to HR since Xander is an employee of the hospital. I suspect our HR will talk to your HR department, Charlotte. Even though you and Damon aren't employees of the hospital, you signed our agreement to follow all our rules. There will be consequences, but for right now, I want you both to take the next two days off."

"That's unnecessary," I insist.

"Not negotiable, Charlotte. Until HR can handle this, you two don't need to be anywhere near Damon. You are not to set foot on the hospital premises. Do I make myself clear?"

Xander and I nod.

Dr. Sear calls HR, and about an hour later, we can finally leave his office. Security escorts Xander and me to the locker room while Dr. Sear makes sure Damon is in his surgery and nowhere near the locker room.

When I get out of the hospital, Xander is right behind me.

"You don't need to follow me."

"I'm walking you to your car, and nothing you say will stop me."

I roll my eyes. "Fine."

We trudge to the car in silence. "I'm sorry I got you into this mess," I tell Xander when we get there.

"Don't you dare apologize to me. Damon did this, not you."

I don't respond. Part of me feels responsible for Damon's bad actions.

Xander opens my door and kisses me on my cheek. His eyes are full of pain and frustration. "Have a good night, Charlotte." His jaw tightens, and he looks away from me.

"Xander."

He looks back at me.

"Get in. I'll drive you home."

"You don't have to."

"Get in."

He lets out a big breath. "Okay."

In the car, Xander fastens his seat belt. "Why didn't you tell me you texted him last night?"

"What good would that have done?"

"We could have gone to HR this morning."

"Right. Because that was super fun and not embarrassing."

"Having your underwear thrown at you is more fun and less embarrassing?"

I jerk my head at him. "Seriously? You think I wanted that?"

"No. Of course, not. That's not what I'm saying."

"What exactly are you saying, Xander?" I sneer.

He lets out a big breath and runs his hands through his hair. "What I'm trying to say is you can't let assholes like that get away with that kind of shit. We should have reported him yesterday."

"Yeah, well, there's a lot of things we should or shouldn't have done yesterday," I hurl at him.

Pain moves across his face, and I have to turn away, once again, blinking back tears.

"You don't know how awful I feel about what happened," he quietly says.

"It is what it is. We just need to move on, Xander."

"Move forward, not move on."

I shake my head. "Nothing has changed. We shouldn't have hung out last night. Let's move on."

"But it has changed."

"You dreamed of fucking another woman. You swore to her she's the only one you'll ever love. I can't even count the times you declared your love for her. In my bed." All the anger and betrayal I've held inside the last six months pours out.

Xander cups my face in his hands. His eyes are glassy. "I know. I hate myself for it. But you don't know the context. It was a missing piece I needed to make things clear."

"So, you remember everything now?"

"No."

I remove his hands from my face, start the car, reverse out of the parking space, and drive through the garage. "I'm not doing this anymore."

"Charlotte."

I slam on the brakes and turn to him. "I can't do this, Xander. I'm sorry, but you have to get out."

"Please, just hear me—"

I begin to cry. "Please, stop. This hurts too bad. I've been dying for six months. Dying."

"I know—"

"No, you don't know! And I can't keep hoping you'll regain your memory. I just can't."

Xander's tears are streaming down his face just like mine, and he tries to pull me into him. "I'm sorry. Please let me—"

"No!" I sob. "Please. Get out. I'm sorry, but please go. I need to stop hurting."

He wipes his tears away. "Okay. If that's what you want."

I drop my head onto my forearms the steering wheel. "It is."

The door opens and shuts. I wait a few minutes, crying into the sleeve of my shirt. When I finally lift my face, Xander is gone.

17

Xander

I'VE BEEN STARING AT THE HOTEL WALL SINCE I GOT BACK. I'M NOT sure how many hours it's been. All I see is Charlotte's face and I hear only the pain in her voice. *"I've been dying for six months... I need to stop hurting."*

Agony strikes through me, over and over, piercing my heart.

My alarm rings, snapping me out of my trance. "Meet with Vivian" pops up on my phone.

Shit. I forgot I'm scheduled to view apartments with Vivian today.

I go into the bathroom, jump into a hot shower, finish, and get changed.

Vivian has texted me an address, and I leave the hotel and hop into an Uber.

I go inside the lobby of the building, and Vivian is waiting.

"Hey, Xander." She leans in and hugs me.

I smile at her. "How's your day going?"

"Great. Yours?"

I'm about to lie but mutter, "I've had better."

"Everything okay?"

"I messed up with Charlotte, and I don't know how to fix it," I blurt out.

Shit. Xander, shut your mouth.

Vivan gapes at me a moment.

"Sorry. I shouldn't have said anything to you."

Vivian grabs my arm and pulls me over to a grouping of chairs. "Sit."

I sigh but obey.

"Tell me what happened, Xander."

She'd never understand. "I can't. It's too bad."

She puts her hand on mine. "I've known Charlotte forever. Better than Piper or Quinn. I've been her only consistent person in life. Tell me."

Nervously, I mutter, "I hurt her."

"How?"

"We've been in the same surgeries."

"I heard." Vivian pauses for a moment. "Xander, do you remember Charlotte?"

. . .

155

"I DREAMED OF HER EVERY NIGHT SINCE THE ACCIDENT, BUT SHE was faceless. Then, last night, when I got to her apartment, I remembered making her pancakes in her kitchen."

"You went to her apartment last night?"

"Yes."

"And you've made her pancakes?" Vivian asks like she doesn't believe me.

"Yes."

"So you remembered? That's good, isn't it?"

"I don't remember everything else. But we got past that and then..."

"Then what?" Vivian asks me quietly.

Blowing out a big breath of air, I admit, "I had a dream about when Billie and I broke up, and I talked out loud in my sleep. Charlotte was sitting in the chair, crying, when I woke up, and she told me to leave."

"What exactly did you say in your sleep?"

"God, this is embarrassing."

Vivian squeezes my hand. "Xander, tell me."

"I may have been having sex with Billie and saying I love her in lots of different ways." I cringe when I say it.

"In Charlotte's bed?" Vivian cries out.

I put my face in my hands. "I've only dreamed of Charlotte before last night. And in the dream, Billie and I broke up. It made everything clear, but I was in love with Charlotte, and not Billie, before I even had the dream."

"You're in love with Charlotte."

"Yes."

"Not Billie?"

"I am not in love with Billie," I stress.

"What did Charlotte say when you told her?"

"She wouldn't let me tell her what the dream was about, and she kicked me out of her car when I was trying to explain."

"When was that?"

"After we talked to HR."

"HR?"

"Damon has been harassing her, and we had to report him today, so Charlotte and I got two days off work."

"Damon is harassing her?"

"Yes. How did she ever date that douchebag?"

Vivian wrinkles her brow. "We only met him a few times, but he was really into Charlotte and seemed fine."

My gut churns at the thought of him *really into* Charlotte.

Vivian laughs. "Don't get jealous now."

I growl, "He's a dickhead."

Vivian stares at me for a minute. "Xander, tell her you love her."

"I tried to explain everything to her, but she told me she needs me to leave her alone. I've caused her too much pain."

Vivian shrugs. "You did."

"I swear it wasn't intentional."

"You don't know what she went through."

"Tell me."

Vivian presses her lips together.

"Please. I want to know."

"Limbo. She lived in limbo between grieving for you and keeping hope alive that you would come back to her. She loved you and probably still does."

Closing my eyes, I think of last night when she told me never to give up hope.

And that's when I vow no matter how long it takes, I'm never going to give up hope we will be together. Charlotte didn't give up on me, and I'm not giving up on her.

Vivian stands up and smooths her skirt. "Come on. Let's go see these apartments."

―――――

A FEW HOURS LATER, AND I'VE MADE NO DECISIONS. EVERY apartment I view, I think, "Would Charlotte like this one?" I think of our text messages, where she agreed to come look with me.

Vivian and I finally go our separate ways. I decide to walk back, and it begins to snow.

Charlotte's voice pops into my head. "I wanted to ice skate in the winter, but we had to stay on the grounds of the orphanage after school."

I stop moving, trying to remember when she told me that.

Her face pops up, and I realize it was during one of our FaceTime calls. She was sitting propped against her headboard, swathed in blankets, her nose was bright red from a cold.

"When I'm in Chicago, the next time it snows, I'll take you ice skating," I told her.

"Really? You ice skate?"

I laughed. "I'm a horrible ice skater, but I'll risk it for you."

Someone bumps into me, knocking me out of the memory, and I realize I'm standing in the middle of the sidewalk.

I get back to my hotel, grab gloves and a scarf, and take an Uber over to Charlotte's. A woman carrying her chocolate-brown poodle leaves the building, and I grab the door before it shuts.

Please be home.

Too antsy to wait for the elevator, I climb the stairs and am soon outside her door. My mouth goes dry, and my pulse increases from nerves, but I knock as loud as I can.

The sound of the dead bolt unlatching hits my ears, and the door swings open. Charlotte's eyes are puffy and red, and my heart bleeds again.

"Xander—"

"Get warm stuff on. It's snowing, and we're going ice skating."

She freezes.

I don't wait for an invitation but step inside and shut the door behind me. "Come on. I promised you. Let's go."

"That wasn't in a text message," she says quietly.

I nod. "I know. It was on FaceTime, and you were curled up in bed, sitting against your headboard."

"What else do you remember?"

I search my memory. "Nothing else because some guy almost knocked me over."

She furrows her brow at me. "You almost got knocked over?"

"Yep. I really shouldn't stop and stand in the middle of the side-walk. Especially in the snow."

She bites her lip.

I notice she's wearing jeans and a sweater. Good enough for ice skating. I open her foyer closet.

"What are you doing?"

"Trying to find your hat, gloves, and a scarf."

"Do I get a coat, too?" she teases, and I know I'm back in the game.

Feeling better every minute, I find an electric-blue hat, gloves, and scarf on a shelf. I put her hat on her then beam at her. "That hat is the perfect accessory for your eyes."

The sexy blush I love creeps into her face, and I brush my lips against hers in a quick kiss.

She holds her breath.

"What coat do you want?"

"The puffy black one."

I slip it off its hanger then help her into it. I wrap her scarf around her and hand her the gloves. Stepping back, I check her out. "You're missing one thing."

"What's that?"

"Shoes. You can't go in socks."

"Oh."

In the back of her coat closet I find a pair of electric-blue snow boots. "These work?"

"Yeah."

When she's all dressed, I lace my fingers with hers. "Let's go."

"Wait, I need to get my keys and wallet."

"You don't need your wallet."

She rolls her eyes and opens her purse and pulls out a credit card, ID, and keys, then zips them in her coat pocket. "Okay, I'm ready."

I smile at her and clasp her hand and pull her through the door, hallway, and into the elevator. When the doors shut, I lean down to her ear and whisper, "There's only one issue."

She looks up at me. "Issue?"

I nod.

Her brows furrow in confusion.

"I don't know where you ice skate in Chicago."

"You didn't take your tourist map?"

"Sorry, can't say I have one of those."

"You didn't ask for one at the hotel?"

"Nope." We step out of the elevator and walk through the lobby.

"You should. It'll give you a good idea of where everything is."

"I remember you telling me you would be my tour guide." I'm laughing then freeze right next to the door to leave the building.

Charlotte puts her hand on my cheek. "Xander, you remember that?"

"Your voice is in my head, saying it, but I don't have a clear picture."

"We were in New York."

I wrack my brain but can't put anything around the memory. I shake my head in frustration. "I'm sorry. I only hear your voice."

"It's okay. Maybe it'll come to you later."

"This happened when I started remembering other things."

"What do you mean?"

"Pieces of medical school, surgeries I was in, different things I had done with the guys over the years. It just would hit me, and, one day, I just seemed to have the entire picture. Well, not the entire picture," I say the last part full of guilt and wish I didn't have to. I'm worried she'll get upset.

"This is a good thing, then." She pats my hand, eyes full of hope, and I pray I don't let her down.

"I think so." Then, I put my arm around her waist and lead her out of the building. "Is it close enough to walk, or do we need a ride?"

"We can walk."

The snow is coming down in thick, sticky flakes, and it doesn't take long before it covers our hats. We are trudging into the storm, and, when I turn to Charlotte, she has snow-filled lashes.

I stop and pull her into me, bend down, and kiss her. We're in the middle of the sidewalk, snow is coming down hard, people are bustling around us, but at that moment, she consumes me.

Our noses and cheeks are cold, but her lips are warm and soft, her tongue teases against mine, and she's once again in my arms.

She laces her hands together behind my head, and I once again have this sense of the past, but I can't place it and don't even try hard. Desire to be hers forever races through me, and nothing feels more right than Charlotte.

"I love you," I murmur against her lips, and she stops kissing me and looks at me like she doesn't trust my words.

"I do. I only love you. But we'll talk about this later." Before she can say anything, I spin away from her but keep my one arm around her waist, and we tread through the snow.

I faintly see the ice rink up ahead, but the snow is thick, so I'm not positive. I point. "Is that it?"

"Yes," she says.

"Are you a good skater?"

She laughs. "Decent. I wouldn't say good. Probably better than you, based on what you told me."

"That I will fall and may end up having Dr. Sear operating on me?"

Her laughter rings through the air, and my heart swells. "Let's hope that doesn't happen. I think brain surgery should be enough for one year."

"And I even have the scar to prove it."

"Okay. Well, I'm anxious to see your skating skills."

We get to the area where you rent skates, and I pay for two pairs. Charlotte and I sit down on a bench to put our skates on. She laces hers and gracefully stands. I put mine on, stand, and almost fall. I grab her, and she laughs. "I told you I suck at this, right?"

She bites her lip. "You going to be able to do this?"

I will probably fall on my ass fifty times and break every bone in my body, but if you want to skate, then I'll break all my bones for you.

"Yep. Let's go." I grab her hand, and after a few steps, I seem to get the hang of balancing on the blade.

But then we hit the ice. As soon as I step onto the slippery rink, I go flying on my belly.

"Shit," I say.

Charlotte skates around me and crouches down. "Xander, you okay?"

"Yep. Good thing I don't have any ego around my skating skills, or I'd be crushed right now."

Charlotte throws her head back and laughs.

I'll fall all night if I get to see that.

She grabs my hand and attempts to help me up, but I'm a lot bigger than her, and I end up pulling her down on top of me.

"I'm sorry!"

She laughs more.

I'm sprawled across the ice, and Charlotte is on top of me. I kiss her, as people skate all around us.

The ice may be freezing, but Charlotte stokes a fire within me, and I'm once again unaware of anything besides her. I harden against her and pull her as close to me as possible.

She pulls back and murmurs, "I'd better get off you before the kids have nightmares."

I give her another peck. "Okay, let's attempt this."

She gracefully bounces up, and I fumble but finally stand.

Once I take a few glides, I lose my balance but catch it then get the hang of it.

I'm not graceful like Charlotte, but I am making progress.

"You've got it now," Charlotte praises as she continues to skate around me.

"Why do I feel you're holding back?"

She grins and shrugs.

"Show me what you would do if you weren't babysitting me."

"Babysitting you?"

"Yeah. Go on. Show me your skills."

"My skills?"

"Yes. I want to see your skills. Go."

"All right."

She takes off and skates several dozen feet then jumps, lands, and spins around like a professional skater.

You've got to be shitting me.

When she stops spinning, she skates back to me.

"That was incredible! Where did you learn to do that?"

She winks at me. "I could tell you, but I'd have to kill you."

"Seriously, where did you learn that?"

"I took lessons when I got my first real job."

"You skate like a pro," I gush at her.

She laughs. "Let's not go overboard."

"I'm not! That was awesome." I'm not just telling her that. It was impressive.

She takes my hand, and we skate together. After a few hours, we decide to turn our skates back in.

The snow is still falling, and it seems to have gotten heavier. "Hot chocolate?" I ask her.

"Sure. There's a cafe across the street if you want to get out of the cold?"

"Yes. That sounds great."

At the coffee shop, I tell her to grab a table while I order the hot chocolate and bring it over to her. I sit down. "That was fun."

Charlotte's eyes crinkle as she smiles. "You're a good sport."

"Hey, I only fell once. I consider that success."

"You did good." She takes a sip of hot chocolate.

We are sitting by the window, and the snow is coming down even harder. "Are we supposed to get a blizzard tonight?"

"Not sure."

"So, what are you doing until Monday?"

She blows on the drink and takes another sip, whipped cream decorating her upper lip. When the tip of her tongue emerges to swipe it off, I almost lose my shit. She can't know how sexy she is.

"I don't know. I wasn't planning on having all this time off."

"Me, either. What is there to do in Chicago in a blizzard?"

She waves around us. "Stay inside."

"Well, that will be boring in my hotel room."

She looks like she wants to say something but stops.

"What?"

She quietly says, "Nothing."

The atmosphere has shifted a bit, and I'm not sure why.

"I saw Vivian today." I wonder if Vivian called Charlotte the minute I left her.

Charlotte blinks at me, surprised. "Why?"

"I checked out some apartments."

A brief look of sadness passes her face, but as quickly as it comes it goes. "Did you find one?"

"No. I kept thinking you were supposed to be there with me."

Charlotte turns and looks out the window.

I stroke her hand, and she sighs and faces me. "I'm sorry I've hurt you."

"I know you are. I'm sorry I kicked you out of the car. Not my best moment."

"It's okay."

"And my house at two thirty in the morning." She nervously gazes at me.

I squeeze her hand. "Charlotte, it's okay."

She looks out the window again and shifts on her seat. I move my chair over next to her and I put my arm around her.

"Don't feel guilty about any of that. Give me one more chance to show you I love you."

"You love me?" She bites down on her lip.

"Yeah. Only you. And I don't want you to say it back until you believe me. Let me show you."

"You don't love Billie anymore?"

"No."

"Do you remember falling out of love with her now?"

"No."

She inhales sharply and bites down on her lip.

My heart rips open again. Charlotte is still hurting and doesn't believe me. I pull her chin to my face and look in her eyes. "It doesn't matter. You're my future. I only want you."

Moments pass, and my heart is beating so loud I'm sure the entire restaurant can hear it.

"I want to believe you, Xander. I do. But I feel like I'm on this roller coaster, and I can't get off."

There's so much pain in her eyes, and I know I've caused it. I'm on the roller coaster, too, and it sucks. I press my forehead to hers and search her blue eyes for any remaining hope she might have for us. "Let's get off it together."

Charlotte

XANDER IS WAITING FOR ME TO ANSWER HIM. MY BRAIN TELLS ME it can't be this easy. That he can't just decide he doesn't love Billie anymore, when he still can't remember falling out of love with her. All he did for six months was obsess over her.

But I'm staring into his eyes. They are begging me to trust him, believe in him, and leap into the unknown with him.

So my heart wins. It overrides my brain, and I lean into the comfort of his arms. There is no rational with Xander. My heart's only desire is for him to love me, and no one else, so I put it on the line once again and tell him, "Okay."

He smiles at me, tightens his arm, and brushes his lips against mine. "Does this mean I get to hang out with you over the weekend?"

I snuggle into him. "You fell on your ass for me skating, so I think it earned you some time."

Grinning at me, he points out the window. There is so much snow coming down you can only see whiteness. "I think we should get going. The snow is pretty intense."

Xander helps me into my jacket and puts my hat on my head again. "You look hot in this hat." He gives me a quick peck on the lips.

It's hard to keep any walls up at all.

He checks his phone. "There aren't any Ubers for over forty minutes. Do you think we can catch a cab around here?"

"Probably not in this snow."

"Okay. You lead then because I have no clue what direction to go."

"I think your hotel is closer."

"Does that mean I get to keep you all night?"

"Do you want to keep me all night?"

Xander gives me a smoldering look. "Is that a serious question?"

I shiver. "You said that and looked at me the same way the night we met."

"What was the question?"

Heat races over me.

"What? Tell me."

"If you wanted to shower with me."

His eyes grow wider, and he licks his lips. "So that's where that dream came from."

"Umm."

He leans down into my ear. "The answer is still yes...about the shower."

Laughing, I shove him away. "Come on, let's go."

We plod through the snow, and I can hardly see. The storm is heavy and wet, and we cling to each other as our feet slip and slide. The sidewalk has a few feet of snow on it, and we take longer to get to the hotel than it should. By the time we get there, we're covered in snow, and our faces are cold.

Once inside the lobby, we shake off our snow and stomp our feet on the mat.

"That was crazy," Xander says.

I shiver from the cold. "I don't think we would have made it to my place. I would have been an official snowman."

"Come on. Let's go get warm." He leads me through the lobby and into the elevator. It's not very crowded, but he pulls my back against him. My teeth are chattering.

His suite overlooks Chicago, and turn-down service has already taken place. Soft music is playing, the fireplace is lit, and dim lights glow.

"Well, haven't you been living it up," I tease him.

He winks at me and goes over to the Jacuzzi tub. It's near the windows overlooking the city skyline. He turns the water on and comes back to me. With a cocky smile, he says, "Time to get you naked."

"Why do I feel like you've always wanted to say that to me?"

Xander laughs. "If I've never said it to you before, then you are correct."

I laugh but shake some more.

"That's my cue," Xander says and pulls my sweater over my head.

"Now I'm colder."

He pulls his shirt off and holds me against his warm skin. "That better?"

"Mm-hmm."

Holding my body to his, he removes my jeans and slides his hands down to my bottom. "You are cold. Come on." He releases my bra and panties and helps me in.

I sit down, the warmth rising to my shoulders, and release a sigh. "Are you coming in?"

"Is that a serious question, too?" Shaking my head, I laugh at him. He strips, tells me to scoot forward, and slides into the water behind me. I lean back on his chest, and he wraps his arms around me.

"This is nice." I turn my head and smile at him.

He kisses me, hardening against my thigh. "Tell me something you've never told me before. Something hardly anyone knows."

Something I've never told him that hardly anyone knows.

There's only one thing that comes to my mind, and no one knows.

Xander is holding me in his arms, and I turn into him more. "I'll tell you something no one knows."

"No one?"

I shake my head.

"Not even Vivian?"

I smile. "Why do you mention Vivian?"

"She told me today she's been your closest friend since you were kids."

"Almost for as long as I can remember."

"But she doesn't know what you're about to tell me?"

"No."

"And Piper and Quinn, they don't know, either?"

"No."

Xander's bright eyes scan mine, and he wraps his arms tighter around me, enfolding me in safety. So I tell him.

"When I was eighteen, and they kicked me out of the orphanage, I got a folder of information about my family."

"They kicked you out?"

"They don't call it that, but it's pretty much what it is."

Xander kisses the top of my head. "Were you scared?"

"Yeah," I quietly admit.

He kisses me on the cheek. "Where did you go?"

"Vivian and I had plans to live together, but we couldn't afford to rent a place, so her parents let me stay with them until we could. The deal was that as long as we were both in school, we could stay."

"Where did you go to school?"

"I had a full ride to the University of Chicago."

"Of course you did, smart girl." Xander beams at me.

"So, when I got my folder, it had relatives listed."

Xander sits up more. "They were still alive?"

I nod.

"But they never adopted you?"

"No."

Wrapping his legs around mine, he pretzels me into his body. "Have you ever talked to them?"

"It was my mother's side of the family. My grandmother, uncle, and aunt are all alive."

Xander tilts his head to the side and squints at me in confusion.

"My grandmother and aunt live together. My uncle lives next door with his family. They didn't know I was coming. I just got in my car and drove there one day."

Xander strokes my hair but says nothing. He puts his lips to my head and kisses my temple.

It's hard to get enough air to continue, but somehow I do. "When I found out, I assumed they must not have known about me because they wouldn't have let me live in an orphanage all these years. I hoped they would want to get to know me..." Uncomfortable emotions creep up, and I focus on the lights outside the window, an airplane passing in the distance.

Xander kisses my cheek.

I turn back to him. "They knew about me the entire time and said my mother always thought she was better than them and ran off with my dad. They wanted nothing to do with me. They said"—I gulp a breath—"I should have died with my parents."

"That's horrible."

"Yeah, it was."

"I'm sorry, babe. You deserved better than what you were dished out."

"I know, but I'm glad I didn't live with them. I guess I got lucky in that matter."

He pushes my hair behind my ear. "How do you do that?"

"What?"

"How do you see so much good in so many messed-up things?"

I shrug. "I don't know. It's better than seeing the bad all the time."

Xander pulls my mouth into his, slipping his tongue against mine, rotating me completely on top of him, and rewrapping his limbs around mine.

"I feel kind of bad," he murmurs between kisses.

"Why?" I lock my hands around his head and get lost in all that is Xander.

"I was just going to tell you how I mutilated all my cousin's dolls."

I jerk back. "You did what?"

Xander shrugs. "I liked to pretend they were hurt, and I had to perform surgery. So I took scissors, popsicle sticks, and string to operate. My aunt wasn't too happy, but my cousin Susie thought it was cool. Well, until she realized her dolls were permanently mangled."

I laugh so hard tears pour down my cheeks. Xander laughs, too. When we finally sober, I say, "I'm glad your skills have improved."

"Amen to that."

"So, you always wanted to be a surgeon?"

Xander's eyes brighten. "As long as I can remember."

"I considered becoming a doctor."

"Why didn't you? You could be. You'd run circles around most surgeons I know."

"I interviewed with my company after graduation. I thought I would try this out, and if I didn't like it, maybe go back. But I love what I do."

Xander smiles. "You're good at it, too."

"Thanks." I stroke his head and trace the scar from his surgery. "Does that hurt when I touch it?"

"No."

I don't know why I say it, I've never told anyone before, but suddenly, it's in my mind. "I only remember pieces of the accident."

Xander sits up more. "Really?"

"Mm-hmm."

He peers at me. "What was that day like?"

"We were happy." So happy.

"What did we talk about in the car?"

I shrug. "We were making plans for when you moved."

Xander strokes my back. "What kind of plans."

I blink several times and quietly say, "You were going to stay with me."

He scans my eyes. "To visit?"

I shake my head.

"Until I found a place?"

"No."

"I was going to move in?"

"Yes."

He smiles. "When did we decide that?"

"When I was in New York. After you took me out to dinner."

"Where did I take you?"

"I don't remember the name, but it was a beautiful place. We didn't eat much though."

Xander lifts one eyebrow. "Why?"

I flutter my lashes. "You couldn't keep your lips off me."

He nods wisely. "I happen to be partial to your lips." He pulls me in and kisses me, positioning me, so my sex is right next to his hard-on, but he stops. "What don't you remember?"

"I remember everything until the crash. Then it's blurry. There was tons of blood and broken glass. Before all the red lights, I kept hearing you moan in pain, but I couldn't turn to see you. Piper and Noah said I called them before I went into surgery, but I don't remember it. I don't remember being freed from the car. I guess I was in shock." I blink back tears then blurt out, "I had nightmares for months after listening to you moan."

"I'm sorry. I'm so sorry you went through all that alone."

Tears well up, and I wish I would stop crying all the time with Xander, but the pain is still so raw. And everything I've been holding back comes out. "I hoped you would recognize me when you saw me, but you looked right through me. You didn't even take a minute to try and remember me."

He cups my face. His eyes are full of pain, just like mine feel. "Charlotte, I'm so sorry. I don't even remember you coming to see me. I was on so many meds, it's just foggy. But that doesn't excuse it. I'm sorry. I wish I could hit redo. I would give anything for a redo."

"I needed you," I whisper. "I needed you so badly."

"I know. I'm so sorry. I'm here and not going away from you ever again. I promise."

I want to believe him. To know for once in my life, I can have someone to love me...someone who I love so much it hurts in so many different ways but is worth all the pain. So when he kisses me and pulls me into him, I allow myself to trust in him and his promise.

"I love you. I'm here for you forever," he whispers against my lips then starts a slow burn within me so hot I don't think and just feel.

My throbbing sex rocks slowly onto him, allowing him to fill me up inch by inch, as I slide against him.

"Hold me tighter," I whisper to him, needing him.

Wanting me.

Protecting me.

Claiming me.

I need it all the way only Xander can give it to me.

He wraps his arms tight around me. Stroking my curves, cupping my ass, moaning, he sends a riptide of flutters coursing through me.

"Always be mine," he murmurs to me, as he lightly sucks on my neck.

"I'm yours." I give myself over, hoping he never wants to give me back.

Pulsing, I push him deeper in me, needing to feel whole. I've only ever experienced wholeness with Xander.

His fingers move between our bodies, and his thumb rubs my clit.

"Xander," I cry out.

"That's it, gorgeous, cum for me." He circles quicker, and I tremble, flying over the edge.

"Oh God!"

"Good girl," he mumbles then moves both hands to my hips and rolls my hips harder and quicker on him.

"Oh jeez," I breath out as he brings me to a new peak and the walls of my pussy spasm.

His lips claim mine as their own, and he pushes his forehead to mine when I can no longer kiss him back.

I gasp for air and stare into his eyes.

"Fuuuuuck," he groans, pumping his seed hard into me, spiking my adrenaline into a sea of pleasure as I climax again, calling out his name.

I collapse, breathing hard, as he grips me to his chest, stroking my back.

We lie in the bath, our limbs entwined. He kisses my head.

He's still in me, and I realize what we just did. I slowly look up at him.

"Don't freak," he says.

"I have an IUD."

He exhales. "Okay. I'm clean."

"Me, too."

He smiles at me and kisses me on the forehead. "I think we just handled that pretty well."

Xander

ANY ASSUMPTIONS I HAD ABOUT CHARLOTTE ARE BOTH CONFIRMED and wrong at the same time.

She is even more incredible than I gave her credit for, and I didn't think that was possible.

She should be broken. Between her childhood, living relatives, and what I've put her through, she should be in victim mode.

But she's not.

Charlotte sees life through a glass half full instead of empty. She needed me, and I wasn't there for her, but she still is willing to love me, believe in me, and allow me to show her I love her.

Charlotte has had no one besides her four friends love her. She could choose any guy she wants, but she's chosen me. And after everything I put her through, she still loves me.

We are naked, lying on our sides facing each other in bed, wrapped up in each other. Her head is resting on my arm, and I am stroking the soft skin of her back.

"When's your birthday?" I ask her.

Sadness passes in her eyes. She quietly says, "February eighth."

I stroke the side of her head. "Why do you seem sad?"

She looks away from my eyes and shrugs. "I don't like my birthday."

"Why?"

"Because it always reminded me that another year went by and chances were going down for a family to adopt me."

My heart bleeds at this moment, thinking of Charlotte as a little girl, waiting for a family who never came to adopt her. I don't know what to say, so I pull her tighter to me and kiss her.

Biting on her lip, she blinks. "I had to hold myself back from texting or calling you on your birthday."

"Good thing you didn't call me because I had a huge pity party that day," I admit.

"What happened?"

I inhale deeply, and my pulse goes up. "Nothing good."

She stares at me, waiting for me to tell her.

"I was really frustrated because I still couldn't remember anything and thought I was twenty-two turning twenty-three. Noah, Chase, and Jamison took me out for dinner and some drinks. The cake came and had thirty-five on it, and it hit me. They'd told me for a month I was not twenty-two, but at that moment, everything hit me. I remembered nothing about the last twelve years, so..." I turn away from Charlotte, not wanting to tell her the rest because of my shame and embarrassment.

Quietly, she says, "It's okay. I won't judge you. What happened?"

"I got drunk and into a fistfight with Chase. Noah and Jamison had to pull us apart. The cops were called because it was in the restaurant, but we all knew the cops from being paramedics. Noah wrote the restaurant owner a big check and convinced him not to press charges. I apparently knew the policemen who were there, but I didn't remember them that night because my memory hadn't come back yet." I wait for her to judge me and rightly so.

But she doesn't. She pulls me closer and strokes my cheek. "It's good you were with friends. That explains a lot now."

"What do you mean?"

"I was still at Noah and Piper's in New York recovering. I assumed something happened, but I didn't know what. Noah acted strange when he came home, but I felt something was wrong. I asked Piper what happened, and she said there was an argument, but everything was fine."

"Things got ugly for a bit after that."

Charlotte stares at me. "With Chase?"

I shake my head. "No, he forgave me before we left the restaurant. It got...it got dark for me."

She scoots closer to me, and our faces are inches apart.

"I...I was frustrated because I couldn't remember. And..." I stop myself from finishing because I don't want to hurt Charlotte.

"And what?" she urges.

I shake my head. "Nothing."

"It's okay. Tell me, Xander."

I lick my lips, and I nervously glance at her. She's waiting for me to tell her. "I kept dreaming of you, and I knew you weren't Billie. So I felt guilty. And I couldn't see your face, so I didn't know who you were. I didn't tell anyone because I thought maybe you weren't real, and I was going crazy." I omit to tell her I considered killing myself a few times before my memory started to come back.

Charlotte says nothing at first. She strokes my cheek. I can see her thinking, and she finally asks, "Do you still feel guilty?"

"No," I say without any hesitation.

"Not even a little?"

I cup her face in my hands. "No."

She lets out a breath.

I lean into her and kiss her, trying to show her she is the only woman I desire and love.

If I could press pause on life and bottle up how Charlotte makes me feel, I would be in a state of eternal bliss. When she kisses me, she consumes me, breathing life into me where I thought I was dead.

When you've gone through the darkness, and you're faced with so much light, it's blinding. People think blindness is always bad, but when you're blinded by light after being in the dark for so long, you realize the things you put stock in, that you assumed you needed to have a future, have been a figment of your imagination.

Charlotte is the light. The blinding light healing me from my fears and all the worries I may never have a clear picture of my past. Whatever happened then can stay there. The only thing that matters is the future.

She laces her hands behind my head, once again giving me a notion of something in the past, some memory that wants to come out, but I don't try to comprehend it. I pull her closer and detach from anything that isn't right now.

My lips move across her jaw, down her neck, and to her chest that is already rising and falling. I lick her areolas, one at a time, teasing her puckered hardness, listening to her quiet whimpers.

Her legs part, widening, so I'm centered on her. My lips give homage to the smoothness of her stomach and the curves of her waist before I feast on her mound.

She moans, and I harden further. Desperation to taste her, as her scent flares in my nostrils, overpowers me, and as I massage her thighs, I take my first nibble.

A perfect concoction of flavors, both salty and sweet, hits my tongue, and I remind myself to take my time and savor her.

"Oh...oh..." she moans, pressing into me.

Gliding my finger in and out of her, I add another, as she grinds harder.

I kiss her inner thighs and around her sex then go back to dining on her, licking her clit, sucking her soft and then harder, flicking my tongue against her delicious, pink pussy.

"Xander," she cries out, bucking harder into my face as I finger fuck her faster.

The heat of her body penetrates my cells, tempting and torturing me, as pre-cum drips down my dick.

"Please...please don't stop," she begs, digging her fingers into my skull and squeezing her thighs around my neck.

I sink my fingers into her hips and pull her into me as close as possible and suck her into her high.

"Xander! Oh...oh!" She flies into a state of glorious ecstasy, vibrating into my mouth and on my fingers.

She's quivering, and when she slows down, I kiss her thighs, letting her breathe, then latch back onto her.

The second time, I ferociously eat her out, and she screams my name, trembling almost immediately into my mouth.

Her flushed skin is warm and smooth, as I make my way up her body. My cock is hard and throbbing, and when my mouth meets hers, she opens her legs and wraps them around me.

I glide into her and groan.

"Oh," she moans, already pulsing around me, bringing my every cell to life.

I stroke her hair. "Keep doing that," I breathe. "You're amazing."

She grasps my shoulders, and her fingers sink into my back. The warmth of her skin melts into mine, and she buries her face in my neck.

Kissing me. Licking me. Sucking me.

Adrenaline is like a spider, weaving its web throughout my body, bouncing from one place to the next, connecting all my cells.

"Harder," she murmurs.

I thrust harder into her as my balls tighten, and I go as deep as I can.

"Oh...Xander," she cries out, and it's the sweetest sound I have ever heard.

"Let go, baby," I tell her. I need her to cum, and I need her to cum now. So I slam into her harder. She spasms violently, shattering in my arms as I release my own hurricane within her.

In our aftermath, I kiss her, keeping my body pressed to hers and not wanting to be anywhere else.

Heaven exists with Charlotte, and I'm a man on a mission to never again forget it.

20

Charlotte

THE SNOW IS STILL COMING DOWN, AND ALL YOU CAN SEE THROUGH the window is whiteness. Xander and I are curled together, warm under the blankets and from each other's skin.

"The guys are coming to town this weekend," Xander tells me.

"That will be nice for you to see them."

"We're supposed to go to Club D. Will you be my date?"

I laugh. "Sure. Am I to assume my friends will be there?"

"Definitely Piper, but I have a suspicion Quinn and Vivian will be there, too."

I nod. "Probably."

"What's going on with those two and Chase and Jamison?"

I roll my eyes. "They claim nothing, but I don't buy it."

"I'm not buying that, either."

"Why do you think they deny it?"

He shrugs. "No idea. But will you go with me to Club D?"

"Yes. Of course."

He smiles. "Good. I'm assuming we're awesome dancers together?"

I beam. "We didn't have any complaints last time."

His hand is on my hip, and he strokes it with his thumb. "How did I first tell you I love you?"

"We just got back from dinner in New York."

"The dinner we didn't eat at?" Xander grins at me.

I laugh. "Yes. You had boxes everywhere because you were packing to move, and you sat on one and pulled me onto your lap. You said, 'I'm madly in love with you.'"

"And what did you say?"

"I said, 'That's good because I'm madly in love with you.'"

Xander looks wistful. "I wish I could remember that."

I giggle, thinking about it.

"What's so funny?"

"I may have done something to you after on that box...before it collapsed." My face heats.

"And what were you doing to me?"

I clear my throat. "Use your imagination."

"It doesn't happen to have the initials B and J, does it?"

"Maybe."

"And the box collapsed?"

I nod. "Right when it was getting good for you."

He burst out laughing. "Okay, now I really wish I could remember that."

I brush my hand through his hair. "Maybe you will someday."

Sadness briefly passes his eyes.

"You okay?"

"Yeah. I just need to keep reminding myself the past doesn't matter, and only the future does."

I stare at him. "What scares you the most about that?"

He hesitates. "You want honesty?"

"Yes."

"It used to be not remembering everything but not anymore."

"What is it now?"

"I'm scared I will go to sleep and have another dream, and I will hurt you. So while I want to sleep with you wrapped up in my arms, I think I need to spend the night on the couch." His eyes drill into mine, full of fear and anxiety.

"You don't have to do that."

"I don't want to lose you, but more than that, I don't want to hurt you, Charlotte."

"I know."

He sits up against the headboard. "When I started remembering things, flashbacks would fly at me during strange moments. I don't trust my mind right now."

I understand what he's saying, but I don't want him on the couch. I want to sleep curled up to him. So many months, I cried myself to sleep or woke up to a pillow soggy with tears because he wasn't here. I don't want to go backward. I cup his face in my hands. "Don't go. If something happens, I'll deal with it."

"I don't want you to have to deal with it. I don't want to cause you any more pain. You don't deserve that."

"We've spent enough time apart. It's fine. I'll be fine."

Xander looks at me, unsure of what to do.

"Stay with me."

"Charlotte—"

I put my finger over his mouth. "There are no guarantees you will or won't have dreams. And it could be forever for all we know. You said we would get off the roller coaster together. This is part of our together."

He takes a deep breath, nervously looking at me, grappling with what to do.

"I'll handle it if it happens."

"You shouldn't have to handle it."

"Stop. Stay." I straddle him and lean in and kiss him, knowing it might happen but telling myself I will have to toughen up and deal with it if it does. I love him, and I want my life to be with him, so if that means we have to deal with his past, then we will.

And I convince myself everything will be okay and that it's just flashbacks and not to let anything bother me, but sometimes things are easier played out in our minds than in reality.

———

I WAKE UP, AND THE DARKNESS IS TRYING TO TURN INTO LIGHT. Xander isn't next to me. I throw his T-shirt on and walk out to the living area. He's sitting in an armless chair, staring, with an expression on his face I haven't seen before. Tearstains are on his cheeks, and he looks like he's seen a ghost. A blanket is wrapped around his shoulders.

"Xander?" I softly say, brushing my hand on his cheek.

He slowly looks up at me.

"What's wrong?"

It's as if it takes him a minute to register who I am? Or maybe that I'm here?

A chill runs through me, and I panic. Did his memory go backward, and he doesn't know me again?

"Xander?" I repeat.

His face changes, and he snaps out of whatever trance he was in.

"Charlotte." His voice holds a hint of surprise in it.

"You okay?"

Nodding slowly, he says, "Yeah."

"What happened?"

"Nothing. Everything is fine." He forces a smile and pulls me into his lap. "Did you sleep well?"

"Yes. Did you sleep?"

"On and off."

"Xander, what is going on?"

"Nothing."

"Please don't lie to me."

He lets out a big breath. "Okay."

I stroke his cheek. "Tell me what happened."

"I've been having some intense flashbacks for the last few hours."

"About Billie?" I do my best to keep it factual with no emotion in it, trying not to cringe.

He shakes his head, blinking back tears.

"What then?"

"Nathan. The first patient I ever lost on the surgery table."

I kiss his forehead. "Nathan was Noah's brother who passed, right?"

He nods.

"Is this the first time you remembered these incidents."

His voice is hoarse. "Yes."

"Do you want to talk about it?"

"No," he whispers.

I pull his head into my chest. "Okay. You don't have to."

His arms wrap around me, and one hand slides under my T-shirt while he looks up and crushes his lips into mine.

I straddle him so I can get as close as possible, trying to show him that any love I have in me I'll give him. I consume his lips, as my knees dig into the sides of his hips, my naked sex against his hardening manhood.

"It seems like it's happening now," he murmurs. His voice is painful and raw, and my heart bleeds for him.

It's a cruel twist from the universe that Xander has to experience grief and pain more than once, and I wish I could take it away from him.

"I'm sorry. What can I do?" I hold him tighter, wanting to change for him what I can't.

"Make me forget. Even if it's just for now." Pain and tears fill his eyes.

I cup his face and kiss him, pouring every ounce of love and desire I have for him into it.

He grabs my hips and slides me over his erection, entering me in one fluid motion.

I sink onto his girth, quivering and gasping as my body accepts him.

"I want to be the man I used to be for you," he murmurs.

"You are."

"I'm not," he insists.

"We're both different, but the same. It's okay."

"You don't deserve this."

"Shh. Don't talk like that." I pull his T-shirt off me. "I want to belong to you. Exactly as you are."

He buries his face in my breasts, licking me, sucking me, owning me.

"Xander," I breath, puckering in his mouth, circling on his cock as he groans.

"You're sunshine," he murmurs and hungrily grasps my head and parts my lips with his tongue, darting in and out of my mouth then yanks my hair back and sucks on my neck.

"Oh God!" I moan as my body hums, rippling and surging with heat.

"I only want you," he whispers.

"Yes," I whisper back.

His eyes drive into my soul. "I will love you forever."

I tremble. "I'll love you back forever."

His arms wrap around me tighter, caressing me, cherishing me, claiming me as his.

It's all I've ever wanted. I've found my heaven in Xander. He fills the holes in my heart I assumed no one ever could. And I want to fill his, so no more heartache ever hurts him again, but I'm not sure how. The only thing I can do is love him, so that is what I vow to do.

"I will be the man you deserve," he murmurs in my ear.

"You already are," I tell him and mean it.

I grind into him harder, needing all of him in me as he shimmies against my walls, creating a tidal wave of euphoria so high in me, I collapse in his arms in tremors, crying out his name.

And as he unleashes his seed into me, he holds me so tight, our orgasms collide, and I no longer can tell where I end and he begins.

I think every second of what we've gone through has gotten us here. That nothing else can happen. That we've done our penance for whatever we've done wrong in this life or previous lives, and now is our time to have it easy, and just be able to love each other.

But love requires unconditional trust. And that isn't always easy to give.

21

Xander

CHARLOTTE AND I SPEND ALL DAY FRIDAY TOGETHER. WE EAT breakfast at the hotel restaurant, and she grabs a tourist map from the front desk to give me a quick overview of Chicago.

After we eat, we buy a deck of cards in the gift shop and spend the afternoon having sex and playing games in my suite.

The snow is still coming down but not as hard. Chase and Jamison will arrive in the early evening, and their flight miraculously isn't canceled.

Around six, we stop at Charlotte's so she can get changed. The guys are staying at Noah and Piper's, and everyone has been invited to their place before we head out to Club D.

Charlotte walks out of her room in a metallic-gold club dress and matching stilettos, and my pants instantly feel tighter. When I whistle at her, the sexy blush crosses her cheeks. I kiss her. "I swear you just get hotter."

She laughs.

I kiss her again. "Maybe we should stay here," I murmur against her lips.

"Ha, ha!"

I step back from her. "You ready?"

She nods, and I hold out her coat and help her into it. Once outside, we catch a taxi and are soon at Noah and Piper's.

As we thought, Quinn and Vivian are over. When we arrive, everyone looks at us in surprise, and I realize no one knows Charlotte and I have reunited. Well, Vivian and Noah know a bit, but they don't know we've gotten back together.

The elephant is in the room. It's quiet, and everyone is staring at us. Charlotte looks at me, and I pull her closer. "Are you going to stare all night?"

Noah smiles and winks at me. "Nope." He walks over and kisses Charlotte on the cheek. "Good to see you, Charlotte."

"Okay, you have some explaining to do." Quinn points at us, and everyone laughs.

Charlotte blushes again.

Piper grabs her hand. "You come with us." She pulls Charlotte out of the room, and Quinn and Vivian follow, but not before Vivian gives me a big smile.

Chase hands me a beer. "You better start talking."

"Hey, guys, nice to see you, too," I sarcastically say.

"Yep. Now spill it." Jamison grins at me.

I wrack my brain, trying to think of where to begin. Noah jumps in. "Charlotte and Xander are at the same hospital."

I nod.

"Do you remember her?" Chase asks.

I start to nod then shake my head. "I remember certain things but not everything."

"That's great, Xander!" Jamison exclaims.

Noah flashes me a knowing look, and I know he's thinking about how I dream about Charlotte, but he doesn't mention it.

"Do you remember other stuff now?" Chase asks, and I know that by other *'stuff,'* he means about Billie.

"A little. Not all of it."

"But enough?" Chase doesn't have to say more. He wants to know if I'm done being obsessed with her.

"Yep."

"Good. It's about time," Jamison mumbles.

I nod. "Any more questions?"

Noah pats me on the back. "No. But we're glad you're finding your way back, man."

———

WE GET TO THE CLUB, AND NOAH'S RESERVED A VIP ROOM FOR US. I haven't found out from Charlotte how badly the girls drilled her, but I can only guess it was worse than what I got.

Inside the VIP room, Piper is sitting next to Noah. Jamison and Quinn are looking pretty cozy, and Vivian and Chase are sitting next to each other. Chase keeps giving Vivian looks like he wants to get in her pants. She looks like she likes him but is trying to keep somewhat of a distance.

I wonder again what is going on with all four of them, but I'm not about to ask.

I've got my arm around Charlotte. Everything seems right. She's laughing and looks so happy, and my heart soars at the sight of her smile.

We've had a few drinks, and I lean into her ear. "Ready to go dance?"

She smiles at me. "Yep."

I pull her up with me. "We're hitting the dance floor," I announce. It doesn't take long before everyone else is standing and following us.

When we get on the dance floor, Charlotte and I easily fall into a rhythm. It's hot and sexy, and our bodies fit together perfectly. The shot girl comes over. I grab two for us, and we throw them back and continue dancing.

A guy comes up to Charlotte and tries to cut in.

I'm claiming you as mine tonight unless you have any objections, runs through my mind as I pull Charlotte into me, making it clear to him and anyone else she's off-limits. Images of her gazing at me, but with pink lipstick, pop up. She's wearing red tonight, and I stop dancing, Visions of her face with both pink and red lips flash so quickly in my mind I almost get dizzy.

"Xander, you okay?" she yells through the music, looking at me concerned.

I nod, but her face is still flashing. "Can we sit down a minute?"

"Sure." She grabs my hand and leads me off the dance floor, through the club, and into the VIP room. By the time we get there, my flashbacks have left.

We sit down. I pull her onto my lap, and she puts her hands on my face. "Xander, what's going on?"

"I'm sorry. Did you wear pink lipstick the night we met? And you wore a pink dress?"

She pauses, thinking. "Yes, I think so."

I nod. "I just had a flashback. And did I tell you, 'I'm claiming you as mine tonight unless you have any objections?'"

She strokes my head and nods. "You did. What else do you remember?"

"Nothing. I don't know if it's because of the lights and music, but your face was flashing between now and then in my head. I'm sorry I ruined our dance."

She puts her finger over my lips. "Shh. You ruined nothing." She leans in and kisses me so sweetly, I'm sure I did something extra good in my last life to have her in my arms.

I pull back and grin at her. "You look hot with pink or red lips."

"Hey, I have to go to the restroom."

"Okay, I'll go with you." I put my arm around her waist and lead her down the hall. She goes inside the restroom, and I stand against the wall, waiting.

I'm looking at my phone when a familiar voice says, "Xander?"

Slowly, I gaze up, not believing it.

"Billie?" I'm in shock as I stare at her. She doesn't seem like she's changed much. Her honey-colored hair looks the same, but I realize she's been drinking pretty heavy when I look at her brown eyes.

"Xander." She flings herself at me, and I catch her in my arms so she doesn't fall.

"Whoa. Steady there."

Before I know it, she grabs my neck, pulls me to her face, and kisses me.

I try to pull out of it, but she is wobbly, so I move my hand on her back to keep her from falling.

She has her hands on my face and on lockdown. I try to pull back, but she's hanging onto me, she's so drunk. When I finally pull away from her, Charlotte is standing in front of me, her eyes wide and blinking back tears.

"Get off me, Billie. Charlotte, this isn't—"

I can't say anything else because her eyes widen farther. She turns and bolts down the hall. Billie is still in my arms, and I try to steady her to go after Charlotte, but she's off-balance, and if I let her go, she will fall.

"Billie, stand up," I tell her sternly.

"Xander?"

I turn to see Sally, one of Billie's friends, staring at me.

"Sally, get her off me," I growl.

Sally looks at me in shock and grabs Billie, trying to steady her.

As soon as she does, I take off down the hall to find Charlotte. I'm entering the VIP room as she tries to get out the door. She has her clutch, and tears are streaming down her face. Vivian and Chase are back in the room, with worried expressions.

"Charlotte, that wasn't what you thought it was."

"Move, Xander."

"No."

She shoves me, and I grab her hands. "Stop. That wasn't what you thought."

"You were kissing...her," she hisses. "Move."

"I wasn't kissing her."

"Get out of my way," she yells as tears stream down her face.

I try to put my arms around her, but she pushes me so hard I stumble back. She slips past me and heads toward the elevator.

I follow her. "Charlotte!"

"Leave me alone, Xander. Once and for all, just leave me alone." Her eyes are full of pain, and my heart shatters.

"You don't know what you saw. Let me explain," I tell her.

The elevator opens. "I know what I saw."

"No, you don't!"

Vivian is suddenly next to Charlotte and puts her arm around her. "Leave her alone, Xander."

I point to Vivian. "Stay out of this."

She scowls at me and steps into the elevator with Charlotte, shaking her head.

"You don't know what just happened," I tell them both.

Charlotte is crying, and Vivian pulls her face into her shoulder, then pushes a button.

I step into the elevator.

"Get out, Xander," Vivian yells at me.

"No. You have this all wrong."

The bouncer puts his arm against the door. "Sir, you need to step out of the elevator."

I reach for Charlotte, but Vivian smacks my hand. "Don't touch her."

"You have this wrong," I sternly say again, looking Vivian in the eye.

"Sir, you need to step out now, or we will remove you," the guard says.

This isn't happening. I step off the elevator. "Charlotte!" I try one more time. Vivian glares at me as the doors shut.

I turn to figure out where the stairs are, but Chase is right behind me. "Xander, just let it go tonight."

"I didn't do anything. It's not my fault. I didn't want that."

He puts his hand on my shoulder and nods. "Let them be tonight. Tell me what happened."

"Billie's here."

"Billie?"

I nod. "She's wasted and practically jumped on me. I held her up so she wouldn't fall, and she grabbed me and kissed me. I tried to pull out of it, and I didn't kiss her back, I swear."

"Shit, Xander."

I rub my palms over my face. "Tell me this isn't happening."

Chase nods toward the VIP area. "Come back into the room."

The elevator opens again, and a few people get off. I step inside. "I got to go."

Chase rides down with me. "Xander, leave her alone tonight. Let her cool off."

Angrily, I glare at him. "Charlotte isn't just a girl to me, Chase. I love her."

"Okay. Still, let her be tonight."

"Advice coming from the king of players himself. Sure, Chase," I tell him.

He snarls, "What the fuck does that mean?"

"Nothing," I mutter.

"No. You said it, so explain yourself."

I sneer. "Okay. Fine. What the hell is up with you and Vivian? Are you playing her like you play all your other girls?"

Chase steps closer to me. "What's going on between Vivian and me is none of your concern. But, for your information, no, I'm not playing her. I like her. And I don't play girls. They all know the arrangement."

I take a deep breath. "I'm sorry. It's not my business."

He pauses for a minute. "Nothing good will come of you going after Charlotte tonight. I'll talk to Vivian. Come back upstairs with me."

I shake my head. "No. I'm done with this place for the night."

The elevator opens, and we step out.

"Okay, then, let me come with you. We'll go grab a beer or something."

"Thanks, but I need to be alone."

Chase sighs. "Don't you think you've been alone enough this year?"

I scoff. "Apparently not."

22

Charlotte

Not only did he kiss another woman, he kissed *her*.

My gut flips so fast I think I'm going to get sick.

We're in the cab, on the way to my place, and tears are streaming down my face. Images of Xander holding her in his arms, bent over, with her hands on his head, and passionately kissing him play like a broken record in my head.

And she's beautiful. There isn't a thing I could say about how she looks to try to make me feel better. She's flawless from her head to her toes.

They looked like they belonged together. She fit in his arms perfectly.

My gut flips so bad I roll down the window, scared I might get sick.

"Char, you okay?" Vivian softly asks.

I shake my head and more tears fall. Vivian pulls my head onto her shoulder, and we say nothing more until we pull up to my building.

When we get into my apartment, I throw on pajamas and come back out to the living room.

"You don't have to stay. I appreciate you coming with me, but I'll be okay. Go have fun with Chase."

"Nothing is going on with Chase and me."

"You keep saying that, but I don't believe it."

"Well, believe it."

I stare at her. "Did something happen between you two?"

"Nope."

"But you want it to?"

"No. He has his schedule of women, and I will not be one of them."

"His schedule of women?"

She sighs. "When you were in the hospital, and Quinn and I stayed with Chase and Jamison, it was pretty clear."

"He had them over when you were there?"

She scoffs. "No. But his phone kept ringing off the hook with them, and one girl must not have gotten the cancellation notice because she stopped by. When she saw me, she commented to him that Thursday was their day."

"You have to be kidding me. She *knows* she's a day of the week?"

Vivian shrugs. "Apparently."

"Damn, Viv. I'm sorry."

"It's fine. We haven't ever been together."

"Yeah, but you like each other."

She shrugs again. "Enough about me. Are you going to tell me what happened?"

My pulse increases, thinking again about Billie in Xander's arms. "I walked out of the bathroom, and he was kissing Billie."

"Billie? As in *the* Billie, he obsessed over for months?" she cries out.

"Gee, thanks for reminding me, Viv."

"Sorry."

Not as sorry as I am.

"How did..."

"I don't know. All I know is one minute Xander and I were kissing. Then I went to the bathroom and then Billie was in his arms. He was leaned over, almost like in a dance pose, and she was gripping his head, and they were lip-locked."

"Ouch," Vivian mumbles.

"Yeah. Ouch."

Vivian is quiet for a moment. "It doesn't make sense to me."

"What doesn't?"

"Xander was adamant he was in love with you and not Billie."

"When did you talk with Xander?"

"Yesterday. We looked at apartments, and he was heartbroken. Or he seemed it. He told me about his dreams and that you kicked him out of your place and car. Oh, and that Damon is harassing you? Why didn't you tell me?"

I sigh. "It all happened this week. It's been a roller coaster."

Let's get off of it together. Xander's voice flies through my mind. My heart rips open wider.

"What did Damon do?"

"Viv, I don't want to get into it right now. Can I tell you about it later?"

"Okay."

After a few minutes, she says, "Char, I know you think you saw what you saw, but are you sure Xander would do that to you? He told me he didn't love her, that he loved you. He was distraught yesterday."

"She was in his arms. He called her Billie. His lips were against hers. What else is there to know?"

Vivian nervously scans my eyes. "I don't know, but maybe you should talk to him. He kept saying you had it wrong. Maybe you do?"

I sneer. "Not quite sure how I could get that one wrong."

Vivian's phone buzzes, and she types to someone, back and forth for a bit. She finally looks up and says, "I think you need to talk with Xander."

"Tell me you aren't texting him right now."

"No, I'm texting Chase. But he said he saw Billie and her friend and that Billie is wasted and you need to talk to Xander."

"Just because Billie is wasted doesn't excuse Xander kissing her!" I snap.

"Chase says she kissed him, and he didn't kiss her back."

"Coming from a guy who cheats on girls with a calendar," I shoot back at Vivian.

She appears slightly hurt.

"What?" I ask her.

"He isn't cheating on them. They know about it. Those girls agree to it."

"That makes it okay?"

She looks at me. "Yes, it does. If they didn't know about it, then fine, but everyone involved knows about it. So he isn't cheating on anyone, and it's not fair for you to say that about him."

She has a point I can't argue with her about. "I'm sorry. I'm just upset and pissed at Xander."

"Maybe he's not to blame for this, either."

A tear slips down my cheek. "Why did it have to be her? Why couldn't he have been kissing some other girl?"

Vivian puts her arm around me. "I know it sucks it was her, but if he kissed someone else, you wouldn't like that, either."

She's right. I don't want Xander kissing anyone except me.

"Char, do you really think Xander would do that to you? I just don't see it."

I only love you. Xander's words roll into my head and cut me like a knife. Do I think he would do that to me? No. But thoughts and reality are two different things, and I learned that a long time ago.

"You didn't see it. I did."

"I know, but don't you think you should at least listen to him first? I don't think you have the entire story."

I'm getting exhausted explaining myself. "I'm not talking to him. I can't keep doing this. For six months, all I've had is constant heartache. I'm so tired of hurting." I cry again.

Vivian hugs me tighter then takes me by the shoulders and looks me in the eye. "Char, do you love him?"

I cry harder and nod.

"Then you need to talk to him."

———

EVEN THOUGH VIVIAN TELLS ME TO TALK TO XANDER, I DON'T. I can't get the visual of Billie in his arms, or her lips pressed against his, or her hands gripping his head out of my brain.

And it gets worse over the weekend.

Now I put Xander's sleeping words with a face.

I see them dating.

I see them kissing.

I see them fucking.

Over the next few days, Xander sends me text messages and tries to call and FaceTime me, but I don't answer or return any of his messages.

"I love you and only you."

"You don't know what happened. I did not kiss her back."

"Charlotte, call me. We've come too far for this to keep us apart."

"You're killing me, Charlotte. Seriously. Please, answer me."

When my doorbell buzzes, I don't answer it. But he must have slipped in when someone left because he is soon banging on the door. "Charlotte, please," he begs through the door and my heart bleeds even more. His voice alone is enough to tear me apart. He finally slips a piece of paper underneath.

CHARLOTTE,

You're my only. I would never cheat on you. Please. We need to talk.

I love you forever,

Xander

I WANT TO OPEN THE DOOR AND LET HIM WRAP ME IN HIS ARMS. But I don't.

Betrayed. That is how I feel, and I allow it to eat at me and guide my decisions.

Is Vivian right and any girl would make me feel this way? Maybe. But the fact it was Billie, the woman he obsessed over for six months, the woman he dismissed me for without a second thought, is extra cruel.

When Sunday comes around, my heart aches so much I decide I need to hear him out, at least let him tell me his side. It's about two in the afternoon, and I bundle up to go out into the cold. I am walking to Xander's hotel, since I haven't been outside in two days, and that's when my heart gets another stab.

About a block from Xander's hotel, through a coffee shop window, I see them. All of them.

Noah, Chase, Jamison, and Xander are sitting in a booth. A chair is pulled up to the end of the table, and Billie is sitting in it.

I freeze, not believing it's her. But it's without a doubt the same woman I saw at the club.

The five of them are deep in conversation, and I don't know how long I stare, as anger and devastation grip me. My chest tightens and I have to remind myself to breathe. Tears fall down my cheeks.

As if in slow motion, Xander looks over at me. He blinks, like he's not sure it's me, then pushes Jamison out of his seat and tries to get out of the booth.

I turn and run down the street and hear him yelling my name. I'm not paying attention, and instead of stopping at the cross-walk, I bolt right through it.

I feel the jolt and see Xander and hear him screaming as I go flying. Then everything becomes dark, then light, then red lights.

"Charlotte," Xander is saying my name. I can't move my neck or my body. Everything hurts. Lights are flashing, and I can hear a lot of people talking about me.

I try to speak, but my words come out mumbled.

"Shh," Xander whispers, as a tear drips onto my cheek, and his hand pets my forehead.

His eyes come into focus, then out, then back in. Everything disappears except for his eyes, and his voice.

Suddenly, I feel like I'm moving, but I can't move my body. "Xa…"

"It's okay, baby. Shh. We're almost there." I feel his hand on mine, and his eyes once again come into focus.

Pain courses through me and I moan and struggle to focus.

"Stay awake, Charlotte. Just stay with me," Xander pleads.

And I try. But the darkness overpowers me.

23

Xander

CHARLOTTE WON'T TALK TO ME OR TEXT ME BACK. ALL WEEKEND I try, but she won't budge. When Sunday comes around, the guys knock on my hotel door and drag me out to the coffee shop.

"Vivian said she told Charlotte to talk to you," Chase claims.

"Well, Charlotte isn't listening." I sink back into the booth.

"Eventually, she has to talk to you. You two work together," Jamison points out.

I shake my head. "She will tell me to keep it professional, I bet. That's what she tried to do last time."

Noah is sitting across from me. "I know that phrase way too well."

I roll my eyes at him.

He turns to Chase. "What's up with you and Vivian? You aren't playing here, are you?"

"Will everyone stop asking me that? I am not playing with Vivian," Chase insists.

"Then what is going on between you two? I don't need Piper upset with me over whatever you're doing with her." Noah scowls at him.

Chase shakes his head. "Yeah, well she refuses to talk to me until Friday, so tell Piper to line up on the list of people pissed at me."

"What did you do?" Noah asks angrily.

"I'm not getting into it. I'm a dick, I need to talk to her; she won't let me until Friday. End of story." Chase looks away hurt.

"What's up with you and Quinn?" I ask Jamison, trying to give Chase a break.

"Another good question. What are you doing, Jamison?" Noah raises an eyebrow in question.

He is about to answer when Noah says, "Keep your cool, Xander."

I soon find out why he said that.

"Wow! I never thought I would find the four of you in Chicago!" Billie beams at us.

I groan, and Noah gives me a "be nice" look.

Billie pulls up a chair next to our booth.

This would be my luck. For six months, I was desperate to find this woman, and now I want nothing to do with her, but she keeps popping up.

I try to think of something civil to say. "Good to see you sober, Billie." I fail.

She waves her hand. "Like I've never had you kiss me when you were drunk. Don't act like a saint, Xander."

I gape in disbelief. "We were dating when that happened, and it was over a dozen years ago."

She laughs. "Big deal."

"It is a big deal. My girlfriend won't talk to me right now."

Billie cringes. "Hey, sorry. I didn't mean to cause any problems. You know how I am when I'm drinking."

Has she not grown up at all in over twelve years?

"Do you want me to talk to her? Tell her I was intoxicated and just having a bit of fun?"

God, no. "No, I do not want you to talk to my girlfriend."

She shrugs. "Suit yourself. So, what are you all doing in Chicago?"

"Chase and I are visiting. Noah and Xander live here," Jamison offers.

"What are you doing here?" I ask her.

"Just visiting. I live out in California now. My husband is a producer in Hollywood."

So that's where she went.

"Wait! You're married, and you kissed me?"

She waves her hand at me again. "I don't know why you're making such a big deal about this. Honestly. We used to do a lot more than kiss."

Noah's eyes widen, and he covers his mouth, stifling a laugh.

"And what would your husband say about that?" I'm not into kissing married women.

Billie throws her head back in gales of laughter. "It's the twenty-first century. Just because you're married doesn't mean you can't have some innocent fun on the side."

This is the woman I obsessed about for six months? I am the biggest asshole on earth.

I suddenly have an immense feeling of gratitude we broke up when we did.

"Innocent fun? Is that what you call it?" I snarl at her.

"Since when did you get so uptight, Xander? You used to be fun, from what I remember. Well, before you got into med school."

I feel nothing but disgust.

Jamison jumps in. "You like California?"

"Yes, it's great. Hey, Valeria has made it big-time. I keep hoping I run into her out in Hollywood but so far no luck. My husband wants to have her in one of his films soon."

Jamison nods. "Yes, she's done well. I think she's booked for the next eighteen months on several projects, so he might want to get in line. She's being selective on her roles nowadays."

"You still with Jennifer, Chase?" Billie asks.

Chase's jaw tightens. "Not in eight years."

"Oh, that's too bad. She was a sweet girl."

Chase snorts, and Noah jumps in and steers the conversation onto another topic as I stop listening.

This stroll down memory lane sucks.

The guys continue to talk with her, and I stare at my napkin. I cannot believe I obsessed over Billie for six months when I could have been with Charlotte.

God, I'm a dickhead.

Charlotte. I need to figure out how to get her to talk to me.

Billie is going on and on about something, and I wish she would leave. I turn to the window, and I see her.

Wearing her blue hat, her blue eyes full of tears, is Charlotte. A lump rises in my throat, and I push Jamison so hard he almost slides onto the floor on his butt. I step on the bench, jump over him, and run out of the restaurant.

"Xander!" Noah calls out as I'm almost to the door, but I don't turn around.

When I get outside, Charlotte is running down the street.

"Charlotte, stop!" I yell, but she keeps running.

"Charlotte!"

She doesn't turn around. The crosswalk light is flashing stop, but she doesn't. A black car plows into her, and as she goes flying, her eyes catch mine.

"Charlotte!" I scream as she hits the pavement hard in the intersection.

I run over to her and pull out my phone, dialing 911.

"Charlotte. Stay with me, baby." I stroke her face and clasp her hand in my other one.

Somehow, Noah, Chase, and Jamison arrive on the scene before the ambulance. They go into paramedic mode, but I'm useless other than trying to get Charlotte to stay awake.

She tries to talk and moans in pain.

"Shh," I tell her and stroke her cheek. "It's okay, baby. Just stay awake for me."

I'm crying. I don't realize it until my tear hits her cheek.

"Xa..." she tries to get out my name, and my heart breaks further.

"Shh," I tell her again. "It's okay, sweetheart. Just stay awake with me."

The ambulance comes and the paramedics immobilize her. I ride with her to the hospital.

"Xa..." she tries to repeat my name, as she blinks over and over.

"It's okay, baby. Shh. We're almost there." I hold her hand tighter and try to get her to focus on my face.

She moans in pain, and my heart once again bleeds.

"Stay awake, Charlotte. Just stay with me," I keep telling her, stroking her cheek and trying to keep it together.

Her eyes flutter and then shut, and I fear I've lost her.

WHEN WE GET TO THE HOSPITAL, THE DOCTOR TELLS ME TO LEAVE.

"I'm a surgeon in this hospital. I work under Dr. Sear."

"I'm sorry, but this isn't your department. You know the rules. Go out to the waiting room."

"No."

"Go, or security will remove you from the premises." The doctor gives me a stern look.

"I'm not leaving her," I say as Noah walks in.

"Xander, you need to come to the waiting room." He puts his hand on my shoulder.

"I'm not leaving here," I repeat.

"I will call security," the doctor warns me.

Noah gets in my face. "You can't do anything right now but come to the waiting room. If you don't go, you'll be kicked out, and that won't help Charlotte. Come on."

I glance at her as the nurse shuts the curtain then Noah leads me to the waiting room.

Jamison is already there with Quinn and Piper.

It hasn't even been an hour, but it feels like a lifetime passes before the doctor comes out. Piper stands next to me, since she's one of her "in case of emergency" contacts.

"She has a concussion, and we are worried about internal bleeding. She has terrible bruising. I'm shocked, but she doesn't have any broken bones. Her left wrist is sprained, and she came down on her shoulder pretty hard, but we didn't find any fractures."

"What about her foot? She was in a car accident this year and had to have it reconstructed."

"Her foot is fine."

"Is she awake?"

The doctor shakes his head. "She is in and out of consciousness. We are trying to keep her awake."

"Can I see her?"

The doctor shakes his head again. "Not yet. We will let you know when you can go back."

"How long will that be?" I ask in a snarky tone.

He gives me a look of mixed sympathy and annoyance. "We will let you know."

Piper puts her hand on my arm. "Xander, come sit down."

I plop into a chair. I don't know what else to do.

I feel a hand on my shoulder. Vivian is sitting next to me. "They kicked me out," I tell her.

She nods.

"I'm a doctor, and they kicked me out."

Several minutes pass, and Chase arrives.

She needs to wake up and stay awake.

Concussions and internal bleeding are dangerous, and a million different thoughts race through my mind.

"Don't go there." Noah snaps me out of my thoughts.

I stare at him.

"Don't," he repeats. "She will be okay."

I stand up. "This is ridiculous. I'm a surgeon in this hospital." I walk away.

"Where are you going?" Chase asks.

"To override this bullshit policy."

Noah is by my side. "Xander, what are you doing?"

"I'm going to talk to Dr. Sear and get access. I'm not sitting in the waiting room any longer. I'm a doctor for God's sake."

"Xander—"

I spin on him. "Stop. I'm going to Dr. Sear, and that's it."

He considers then nods. "Okay. Let me come with you."

"Fine."

I plow through the hospital directly to Dr. Sear's office, past his assistant, and knock. He yells to come in.

"Xander," he says, surprised when I open the door, and his assistant is behind me telling him she is sorry for my intrusion.

Before he can say anything, I blurt out, "Charlotte is in the ER. She got hit by a car, and they can't keep her awake. I need to get into the room."

He stands. "Did they diagnose her yet?"

"Possible internal bleeding, concussion, sprained wrist, and shoulder. You need to help me, so they don't call security. Please."

He pats me on the back. "Okay. Let's go."

"Thank you."

We walk back through the hospital and into the ER unit. Dr. Sear finds her doctor, and, after a five-minute conversation, he allows me to go back, with the agreement, I won't interfere with any decisions the doctors need to make.

Noah pats me on the back, leaves, and goes to the waiting room. I thank Dr. Sear, and he tells me to keep him updated.

I enter Charlotte's room. She's hooked up to all kinds of machines. I know what every device is, what it does, and why she needs it, but when I look at her, I have to blink back tears.

The nurses are on shifts to try to keep her conscious. The one currently in the room I've spoken with several times over the last few weeks during my hospital duties, and I tell her I will take over trying to wake Charlotte. She leaves, and I lean over Charlotte and kiss her forehead. "Charlotte, wake up, sweetheart."

Her eyes flutter but only momentarily.

I kiss her eyelids, one at a time, then whisper in her ear, "Come on. I need you to open your eyes, Charlotte."

She opens her eyes then shuts them quickly.

"The lights are bright, just go slow."

She tries again and moans as she closes them.

"You're doing good. Just keep trying." I kiss her on the lips and stroke her cheek.

"Xander," she whispers with her eyes closed.

I brush my hand across her hair. "I'm right here. Open your eyes for me."

Her eyes open and then shut again. "Bright," she whispers.

"I know, baby, but you need to keep them open. Let me help you." I cover her eyes so they are semi-shaded from the light. "Open your eyes now, and I'll move my hands slowly."

She moans. "Everything hurts."

I tilt my head down so I can see her eyes through my hand. "I know, baby, I know. I need you to open your eyes so you can get better. Come on, Charlotte."

Her eyes slowly open, and this time she doesn't shut them.

"Good girl. Okay, I'm going to move my hand just a little, and it will get brighter. Look at your feet and not the ceiling."

Her eyes shut.

"Open your eyes," I tell her sternly.

She opens them quickly.

"Good. Look at your feet."

She tries to focus on her feet.

"Good. You're doing good, Charlotte. It's going to get brighter."

"Wait," she whispers.

"Okay."

She grabs my hand with hers, shuts her eyes, and brings my hand to her lips.

A tear slides down my cheek, and I wipe it away on my arm. I bend down and kiss her forehead. "You have to wake up, sweetheart. Wake up so I can help you, okay?"

"Mm-hmm," she mumbles.

I put my hand back over her eyes, but I don't shield as much light this time. "Look at your feet, baby."

She opens her eyes and stares at her feet.

"Okay, good. I want you to keep your eyes open, okay?"

"It hurts," she whimpers, and a tear rolls down her cheek.

My heart is ripping through my chest, seeing her in so much pain. "I know. But I need you to keep them open."

"Okay," she whispers.

"Good, Charlotte. You're doing so good." I kiss her on the forehead again and move my hand completely away.

She blinks a few times.

"Keep them open, Charlotte."

She continues to blink until she is staring at her feet. Slowly, she looks over at me.

I bend down and kiss her, stroking her hair. "You're doing so good, baby."

Her blue eyes stare into mine. "What happened?"

"You got hit by a car."

She tries to nod and winces in pain.

"Just lie still." I grab the chair and pull it up next to her.

"Do you remember the accident?"

"No." She looks at me, worried.

I stroke her cheek. "Don't worry. That's normal. It'll come to you later."

"Did I break my bones? My entire body hurts."

"No. You got lucky. But you have a concussion and a lot of bruises."

"Can I go home? I want to go home."

"Not yet. But as soon as I can get you out of here, I will."

24

Xander

It's late at night when Charlotte gets discharged. She only gets released because I sign a waiver saying that I'll look after her and take her as a patient in my care.

They want to keep her for observation, but I can do that, and she keeps saying she wants to go home.

She hasn't brought up Billie, or Club D, or the coffee shop. I don't know what the last thing is she remembers, but I don't want to ask her in the hospital. At some point, it will come back to her, if it hasn't already, and we will have to talk, but now is not the time. Plus, she's on a lot of pain medicine.

Chase and Jamison returned to the airport. Quinn and Vivian took them after they saw Charlotte. It was a quick visit because Charlotte is in a lot of pain and seems to want only me by her side.

Noah and Piper saw her, too, and left a few hours ago, but Noah sent his driver back to the hospital to take us to Charlotte's.

Piper took my hotel key. She packed a bag for me and dropped it off at Charlotte's. I already told Dr. Sear not to expect me for at least a week, so I don't have any reason to have to leave her side.

When we get to Charlotte's, it's after midnight. I carry her upstairs because she's weak and dizzy from her concussion. She nuzzles into my neck and murmurs, "You always smell good."

I smile and kiss her head as the elevator doors open. When I get into her apartment, I take her right to her bedroom, give her a glass of water and her pain pills, then go into her closet and find a pair of pajamas for her.

"I need a shower," she whispers.

"Tomorrow. Just rest tonight."

"I feel gross. I'm going to take one." She tries to sit up and throws her hands to her head. "Ouch."

"Whoa. You need to move slow."

She sits for a minute then stands and ambles into the bathroom.

"Where are you going?"

"Shower," she mumbles.

I follow her into the bathroom, making sure she doesn't fall. I point to her vanity bench. "Okay. Sit down, and I'll get the shower ready."

She lowers herself carefully and winces. "Why does my ass hurt so bad?"

"Because you were hit by a car," I tell her.

She softly laughs.

I join her. "Why are we laughing? It's not funny."

She laughs harder. "I don't know."

I kiss her on the head. "Stay put."

I turn the water on and get naked.

"No offense, Xander, but I don't think I'm up for shower games tonight."

I chuckle and grin at her. "Don't worry. Your virtue is safe. But you can't go in there alone. You'll fall, and even the shower pressure will hurt your bruises."

She smiles at me. "So, you're going to scrub me down?"

"Yep." I undress her, trying to avoid her bruises and lead her to the shower. After I test the water, I step between her and the spray. I hold her against me. "Tell me if you get too hot or dizzy, okay?"

She tips her head back and kisses me on the lips. I try to contain my growing erection, but it's pointless. I can't stand next to Charlotte naked and not have one.

Taking the sprayer, I wet her hair, shampoo and rinse it, then do the same thing with her conditioner.

"The answer is still yes," she mumbles.

"What's that?"

"That you want to shower with me." She grabs my cock and sways.

Realizing her drugs have kicked in, I soap her up, rinse her clean, and turn the water off.

After I dry her, I wrap a towel around her and have her sit on her bench so I can comb her hair. Then, I dress her in pajamas and tuck her into bed.

I climb in next to her, and she giggles then runs her finger down my nose. "Are you sure you remember me?"

I put my face on the pillow, next to hers, and stroke her hair. "Yes. Don't worry about that."

"Do you remember you're a doctor?"

I kiss her. "Yes, I remember I'm a doctor."

"Are you still searching for Billie?"

My face falls. "No. I only love you, Charlotte."

"Good. It's about time you remembered me."

"Yes. I'm sorry I took so long." I kiss her again.

She pushed up on one elbow. "Let's play dirty doctor."

Amused, I lower her to the pillow. "Dirty doctor?"

"Mm-hmm."

"And exactly how does one play dirty doctor?"

She grabs my cock. "You're the doctor, and you get to be dirty while you examine me."

"Yeah? How dirty does the doctor get to be?"

Her eyes light up, but I know it's the medicine. "You get to be very, very, dirty." She squeezes my cock, and I know I'm going to have blue balls all night. "And I have to do whatever you say."

"I'll tell you what. Let's start now."

She claps. "Yay."

"The first thing you have to do is go to sleep."

She pouts. "That's not dirty."

"I'm the doctor, and I'm in charge. My patients who do what I ask get very dirty examinations when they least expect it."

"Hmm. I feel like you're tricking me." She squints at me.

"Oh, but I'm not. Filthy, full-body, examinations are only for my patients who go to sleep."

"And you sure you aren't tricking me?" She yawns.

"I'm not tricking you." I will definitely cash in on this when she's not all drugged up and in pain.

She smiles at me. "Okay. I'll go to sleep, then. But I want you filthy."

"I'll be really filthy with you."

She closes her eyes and says, "'Don't forget, I love you, Charlotte,' you told me. Then I said, 'I won't. Don't forget, you love me.' But then you forgot me."

I don't know if this is the drugs talking or something that happened, so I ask her, "What are you talking about?"

But she's already asleep, so I wrack my brain all night wondering if it really happened or not.

———

"XANDER, I CAN'T MOVE. CAN YOU MOVE?" CHARLOTTE SAYS IN A panicky voice.

I wake up and realize she is talking in her sleep.

"Xander, talk to me. I can't move. Please. I'm scared."

Putting my hand on her cheek, I stroke it. "Charlotte, wake up."

"Xander," she cries out louder, and tears fall down her cheeks.

"Sweetheart, wake up." I wipe her cheek with my thumb.

"Xander, please, say something," she sobs.

"Charlotte, wake up." I raise my voice and rub her shoulder.

"Xander," she sobs louder.

I pull her into me. "Charlotte, come on. You're dreaming."

She slowly opens her eyes and relief fills them. "Xander," she sobs and wraps her arms around me.

"Shh. It's okay. Everything is okay." I kiss the top of her head and hold her tighter, trying not to hurt her bruises.

"I can't get it out of my head," she cries.

"What's that?" I whisper.

"The accident. I can't get it out of my head."

"I'm sorry. I'm so sorry." Guilt shoots through me that she remembers it, and I don't. Not that it would stop her nightmares, but it doesn't seem fair.

I scoot back down on the bed and hold her in my arms, stroking her hair until she falls back asleep. I glance at my phone to see what time it is and see she has another few hours till her next dose of medicine. My alarm is set, but I don't sleep.

So much has happened in the last week.

It's only been a week.

In that time, I found Charlotte again, and I can't lose her. When she's not drugged up and feeling better, we need to talk. I need her to understand I will never have eyes for anyone but her—she is my everything.

I wonder if she will wake up tomorrow and everything that happened at Club D and the coffee shop will come flooding back.

Better to tell her first chance you get, so when she remembers it, she doesn't flip.

I vow, as soon as she is not heavily medicated, that I'll tell her exactly what happened. I only hope I get to tell her before she remembers it again and freaks.

25

Charlotte

Xander is still moaning, but we are moving.

Why are we moving? Where am I?

A stranger, a man I don't know, is looking down at me.

"You're doing good, Charlotte. We're almost there."

"Xander?" I call out, but all I hear is his moans.

"He's right here. Just stay awake for me," the strange man says.

I can't move my neck, but I roll my eyes to the side and see Xander's body. I see his face, but he's in a neck brace, and a woman is hovering over him. His eyes are shut, and he keeps moaning, as if in pain.

"Xander," I whisper and feel a tear run down my cheek.

"Charlotte, wake up," I hear Xander say.

"Xander?" I try to look at him, and this time I can move my head.

He puts his hand on my cheek. "You were dreaming again."

Closing my eyes, I think about my dream. I open them again. "We were in the ambulance."

He nods. "I think your concussion jostled some memories of our accident. You've been having nightmares all night."

I try to sit up, and it's like someone is taking a hammer to my head.

"Whoa. Easy," Xander instructs.

"Why do I hurt so bad?" I ask him.

"You got hit by a car yesterday."

My eyes fling open as memories of Club D and the coffee shop come hurling at me.

"Billie," I whisper.

Xander cups my face. "You need to listen to me. Nothing is going on with Billie and me. I don't love her. I did not kiss her. She was drunk and about to fall. I did not know she would be in the coffee shop. I have zero feelings for her. I only love you."

I scan his eyes, back and forth, so quickly I get dizzy.

"You're on a lot of medication right now. We will talk about this later. All you need to know is that I only love you." He brushes his lips against mine then takes the glass of water and a pill from the table. "Take this, or your pain will get a lot worse."

I swallow the pill and water.

Maybe it's because I'm in pain. Perhaps it's because I can't think straight. Whatever the reason, I let the thought of Billie fall out of my mind.

"Where do you hurt?"

Where do I hurt?

"My head...my wrist..." I glance down to see my wrist wrapped up in a brown bandage. I turn toward Xander, a little too fast and my head spins.

"Move slowly," he tells me.

I study the bandage. "Did I break my wrist?"

"It's only sprained. Everything is okay." His voice is soft, and he brushes my hair off my face and kisses my forehead.

"Work. I have to call work."

"Shh. They already know. Don't worry. Just rest." He pulls me into his arms, and I rest against him, drifting in and out of sleep. Every time I wake up, Xander is there, giving me medication, trying to get me to eat or drink, and holding me.

A few days of fogginess pass, and I wake up. The sun is beating in my window. Xander is sleeping beside me.

He looks peaceful, and I wonder how much sleep he's had and what day it is. I ease free of his arm and sit up on the side of the bed. My phone tells me it's Wednesday and past noon.

Has he been here since Sunday?

I stand slowly, walk into the bathroom, and turn on the shower. A faint memory of Xander combing my hair flashes through my mind.

I try to remember where it came from, but I can't.

While the water is warming up, I brush my teeth, remove the wrap on my wrist then undress. I step into the shower and cry out as the water hits my back. I step forward, out of the way of the water.

Why did that hurt so badly?

"Charlotte, you okay?" Xander's voice rings through the shower.

I turn behind me, and his face pops around the glass door.

"Why does the spray hurt my skin?"

"Your back is bruised from when you hit the ground." He strips and steps into the shower.

I'm confused. He pulls me into him. "Come here, sweetheart. Let me help you."

He grabs the sprayer and wets my hair.

Déjà vu hits me. "Have we done this before?"

He squeezed shampoo into his palm. "Yes, when you first got home from the hospital."

When I first got home? On Sunday?

"I haven't showered since Sunday?" I ask, horrified.

He works the shampoo into a lather on my hair. "Nope."

"Yuck. I'm sorry."

"There's nothing to be sorry about. You've been sleeping."

I let him wash and condition my hair, but images of him kissing Billie come into my mind. When he's done rinsing my hair, I stare at him. "We need to talk, Xander."

"Yeah, we do but not just about what happened."

Confused, I tilt my head at him. "Besides your ex-girlfriend who you've obsessed about, locking lips with you, what else do we need to talk about?"

"Words with Friends." He searches my eyes.

"Words with..." He knows it was me. I take a deep breath.

"The Damon situation."

The Damon situation? What is there to talk about? Must be whatever HR did to him.

Xander turns the water off and gently dries me, being careful of my bruises. He grabs the robe hanging on the hook and helps me in it then towels himself off and wraps it around his waist.

"Go sit at your vanity."

I say nothing and sit down. A million thoughts race through my mind, going back over all the conversations we had while we played Words with Friends.

Shit, shit, shit!

He combs my hair, wraps my wrist in a new bandage, and kisses me on my forehead. "I'm going to put some clothes on. I'll bring you some clean pajamas."

"Xander—"

He puts his finger over my mouth. "Get dressed, and then we'll talk."

We both quietly change.

"You hungry?" he asks.

I nod.

"Okay, let's go." He takes my hand and leads me out to the kitchen. He pulls out the barstool. "You want to sit here or on the couch?"

"This is fine."

He pulls food out of my cabinets and fridge. I watch him, not sure what to even say.

I spent months talking to him, never revealing who I was. I lied to him and told him we didn't know each other. I even told him to consider our conversations a safe zone.

Shit.

As I watch Xander make breakfast, the pit in my stomach grows. I should have told him the night we played Scrabble.

He dishes up food for us both then comes over and sits down next to me.

"I'm sorry," I blurt out.

"Wait. Eat first. I'm switching your medication over. The stuff they have you on is super addictive. You need to eat to take the new medication."

He pulls me onto his lap, and like the first night we met, he feeds me a bite of a pancake.

After I chew and swallow, he leans in and kisses me. It's just a small peck, but it's enough to confuse me. "Are you not mad at me?"

Xander shakes his head. "No. Why would I be mad?"

"I lied to you for months."

He nods. "Yeah, you did, didn't you?" He puts another bite of pancake in my mouth.

I chew, swallow, and say, "Why aren't you mad?"

He hands me my pill and a glass of water. "Take your medicine."

I obey then ask him again, "Why aren't you mad?"

He continues to feed me. "Because I needed you, and you were there for me, even though I didn't know it was you. You were light for me in my darkness."

My heart beats harder. "I thought you said you were past the darkness when we first started playing again."

He slowly shakes his head. "It still was popping up. It just wasn't as often."

"So you aren't mad that I lied to you?"

"About that, no."

I search his eyes. "Why do I feel like you are accusing me of something else?"

He lets out a sigh. "I'm not accusing you of anything, but I think you've missed telling me about some big details regarding Damon."

What is he...? Oh God. My gut drops, and I turn away.

He puts the fork down and cups my chin, bringing me to face him again. "Charlotte, why didn't you tell me?"

Blinking back tears, I tell him, "I don't want to talk about it."

How did he find out?

"Charlotte—"

I cut him off and stand up. "No. I'm not talking about it."

Xander takes a deep breath. "You have to talk to me about it. It's out there."

The hair on the back of my neck stands up. "What do you mean, it's out there?"

"He sent it to HR. He is using it to claim that you were harassing him and wouldn't leave him alone after you broke up."

"I don't understand. What did he send?"

Xander's eyes widen. "You don't know?"

My entire body goes clammy. Whatever Xander knows that I don't, it's not good. "What?" I whisper.

"The video."

"The video?"

"Did you not know he recorded you?"

Any remaining blood drains from my face. "What?"

"And it's dated two months ago?" He pushed hair off my face.

I turn away and close my eyes, not able to bear looking at him. My stomach pitches, and I bend over, trying to stop the nausea.

"Charlotte, come sit down." Xander leads me over to the couch.

Why is he calm about this?

I lean over and put my head between my legs. Xander wraps his arm around me and rests his hand on my hip.

This cannot be happening. I sit up. "What is on this video?"

A sympathetic expression crosses Xander's face.

"Have you seen it?" I whisper.

"HR emailed it to you, and it popped up on your phone."

My eyes widen in horror, and I shake my head. "No."

He pulls me into him, but I push him away. I stand and go to my room.

"Charlotte—"

I turn back to him. "I want you to leave, Xander."

"No. I'm not leaving."

"Go," I yell at him as tears stream out of my eyes.

He steps closer to me. "I said I'm not leaving."

"Get out," I cry, as embarrassment, anger, and shame all drive through me. And it's not only at Damon, or myself. It's at Xander as well.

Xander pulls me into his arms. "I'm not going anywhere."

"You didn't remember me. You told me all about her and how you've only ever loved her," I sob into his chest, pushing against it with my fists. "I thought you were never coming back to me, and I needed you. I was so alone."

He holds me tighter. "I'm so sorry. I know I wasn't there for you."

"I didn't even know he was coming over. I just wanted to feel something besides pain," I cry into his chest.

"Shh. It's okay." He kisses the top of my head.

"How did he record me?" I sob.

"I don't know, sweetheart. I don't know," he murmurs.

I pull away. "I need to see it."

Xander sighs and looks at me then hands my phone to me with the email.

"Can you go into the other room, please?" I ask.

"I will, but I'm not leaving now or after you watch it." He shuts my door behind him.

I go and sit on the bed. I feel sick but know I need to watch it. I push play, and it starts. When it ends, one thing is clear. Damon has stripped the audio and made it appear like things went further than they did.

26

Charlotte

Two Months Earlier

NEPHRIC, XANDER PUTS DOWN ON THE BOARD AS THE SCREEN tallies the total and claims he wins.

"Finally!" comes across the chat box.

I laugh. "You were kind of overdue."

"Ouch!" he writes back.

We banter back and forth a bit. And because I have to torment my soul, I ask him, "Have any new memories about Billie popped up?"

"No. My friends keep trying to tell me I don't love her."

I don't respond for a minute. I know I need to stop playing with Xander every night and talking with him, but I can't. I'm addicted to playing with him and keeping him in my life. I miss him so much, and our conversations sometimes fill a hole in my heart and at others, rip it open wider.

Tonight, it's ripping it open wider. But I have to continue asking him. The ache I feel for him is worse at times, but I continue the destruction of my heart.

"What do you think?"

"She's the only woman I've ever loved and the only one I ever will. It would be impossible for my friends to be right."

Tears stream down my face. It's not a different story from any other night, but it hits me really hard.

What if he never really loved me?

No, he did.

Did he really?

As my mind plays games with me and my heart shatters, my doorbell rings. I'm not expecting anyone. "Hello?" I say into the intercom.

"Hey, it's Damon. I heard you're back. I brought some dinner over."

Damon? He wasn't exactly nice when we broke up. What is he doing here?

Against my better judgement, I buzz him in. When he gets inside my apartment, he's holding bags of food and says, "Charlotte, have you been crying?"

I rub my fingers on my cheeks, trying to wipe the stains away. "I'm fine. Just had a bout of pain."

He pulls me into his arms, and even though it isn't Xander's arms, it's comforting to have someone hold me. It's been so long since

I've had any contact with anyone. I've been avoiding my friends and making excuses not to allow them to come over. I've even not answered the door when they've showed up unannounced.

Damon kisses me on the head. "Go get comfy on the couch. Let me fix you a plate of dinner."

If I had been thinking straight, I never would have let him into my apartment. I would have listened to my gut say, "Don't let him in." Damon revealed his not-so-nice colors when I broke up with him, and the things he said to me I wouldn't ever forget.

But here he is, bringing me dinner and trying to comfort me.

Maybe I'm wrong about him?

He's not Xander.

You need to get over Xander. He's over you.

Damon goes into the kitchen. I need to use the bathroom so I excuse myself. When I return, I'm heading for the armchair, but he says, "No, sit on the couch."

My gut asks me why, but I don't listen and go sit on the couch.

"Here, have a drink."

I don't think and drink it. I cough, as the hard alcohol burns my throat. I put it down on the table.

"Jesus, Damon. There's no mixer in this. It probably has three or four shots in it."

Damon picks up my glass and hands it to me. "It'll help your pain. Just take another sip."

Please put me out of my misery.

I take another sip then blurt out, "Why are you here? We don't exactly hang out? You said you hated me."

"I'm sorry. I shouldn't have said that." He leans into me. "I don't hate you."

The buzz of the alcohol works its way through me. I don't even think about the fact I'm on pain medication and shouldn't be mixing any alcohol with what is already in my body.

"You don't hate me?"

He shakes his head. "No. I'm sorry I was such a dick. I came over to be your friend. Can I just be your friend right now?"

If it was any other day, I would be cautious. But the combination of Xander declaring his love for Billie again, the emptiness I've felt for so many months, and all my sadness, don't allow me to be. I fall for his trap.

"I would like that." I look into his eyes.

"Good." He hands me my glass and picks up his. "To friendship." He clinks my glass and we both drink.

The burn of the vodka runs down my throat and into my empty stomach. Maybe this is what I need to feel better.

We joke around for a bit and continue to drink. The food stays in the kitchen. It's been so long since I've talked to anyone. Since I've been ignoring the girls messages, the only person I've been having conversations with is Xander, and that is only through messenger.

I don't know if it's because I haven't drunk since before the accident, or because I haven't eaten all day, but suddenly, I'm feeling better than I have in a long time. And it feels good to feel happiness, even if it is a false happiness from the alcohol.

Damon runs his finger from my lips, down my chest and stomach, stopping right above my mound. "Friends help each other out, don't you think?"

My chest heaves. I know what he's implying, and I should tell him to go, but I need to feel something besides pain. I think of Xander and how he's searching for Billie, not thinking anything about me, while I wallow in heartbreak.

Maybe Damon isn't so bad after all? Maybe I should give him another chance? Maybe I'll be able to forget about Xander?

"Yes," I breathe.

Damon leans closer, puts my glass to my mouth, and I take a sip. The burn of the alcohol once again runs down my throat and I cringe, but he gives me another sip.

This isn't what you want. Tell him to leave.

What you want is Xander and you can't have him. Wake up and stop holding onto hope for someone who feels nothing for you. At least Damon wants you.

His lips move next to mine. "You want some heat, Charlotte?"

Heat. It's what I told him we didn't have.

I stare into his eyes, paralyzed, not sure how to respond.

He laughs. "I'm ready to give you some heat. You want some?"

Xander is heat.

Xander doesn't want you.

As if in a trance, I nod.

"Tell me to fuck you, and I'll give you so much heat your head will spin." Damon's lips are still next to mine, and he is stroking my womanhood that hasn't been touched in months.

Without thinking, I whisper, "Fuck me."

"No. Say it louder, and say my name."

"Fuck me, Damon," I say, louder.

He smiles. "No. Tell me again, baby, but louder."

I repeat it, louder, and then again, laughing, feeling the effects of the alcohol and all the loneliness and heartache of so many months.

"Good girl," he praises and has me drink more. "Now, stand up and strip for me, while you tell me to fuck you.

This is messed up.

Strip for you?

Just pretend he's Xander.

I'm no longer thinking about anything logical. I'm so buzzed, he has to help me stand.

In a wobbly state, I tear my shirt off. "Fuck me, Xan...Damon," I correct myself, laughing.

The room is spinning.

"Take your bra off."

I struggle to release the clasp in the back because I'm so drunk. He comes over and releases it and then sits back on the couch and I throw it at him.

"That's my girl."

"I'm not your girl, I'm Xan—" I stop myself and just laugh. "Actually, I'm no one's girl."

"But you want to be?"

I nod. "Yeah."

"Okay, baby, you're going to be my girl."

"Yours?"

"Yes."

I laugh. *Who gives a shit at this point?* "Okay, I'll be your girl."

He stands and brings his drink to my lips. It burns down my throat.

He laughs. "You want some heat?"

I nod. "Yeah, I want heat."

"Say, 'Damon, I want to be your girl,' and I'll give you heat."

"Damon, I want to be your girl," I say and grab his arm so I don't fall.

"That's my girl." He beams at me, and my ego soars from his praise. He stabilizes me and says, "Now, take your pants off."

I release my pajama bottoms and they fall off me.

He reaches down and helps me remove them past my walking cast. Standing back, he instructs, "Get those panties off."

I just shimmy out of them.

He sits back down on the couch. "Say, 'Fuck me, Damon,' and I'll give you so much heat you won't be able to walk tomorrow."

I laugh. "I already can't walk."

"You want heat though, right?"

I shake my head.

"No?"

I shake my head again. "That's not what I really want."

"What do you really want?"

"To forget."

"About what?"

"Not about what. About who."

A strange look crosses his face, but I'm so inebriated I can't decipher it and don't really care.

"Say, 'Damon, fuck me,' and I'll make you forget."

I don't hesitate. "Damon, fuck me."

Louder.

"Damon, fuck me," I say louder.

"Beg me."

I throw my head back laughing. "You're so messed up. Everything about you is screwed up."

"Isn't that what you love about me?"

Nope. I've never loved you.

"Sure." It's easier to just say what he wants to hear.

"So, beg me, and I'll make you forget."

What the hell? This is messed up. Is it any more fucked-up than Xander wanting Billie?

I get on my knees and crawl between Damon's knees, I stare him in the eyes and say, "Please fuck me, Damon."

"Bitch, suck my dick."

Bitch?

Xander would never do this to you.

This is stupid and not what I want or need.

I'm over this game.

"Suck your own dick, Damon," I slur.

He grabs me under the arms and pulls me onto his lap so I'm straddling him. "Let's not get nasty now."

What the heck am I doing?

"This is a bad idea. I'm done."

He laughs. "No you aren't."

I stare at him in the eye. "Yeah, I am. I don't know what I'm doing. You need to leave."

"You're such a tease." He grabs my head to kiss me.

I push out of his grasp, and grab the blanket off my couch, wrapping it around me. "Just leave, Damon."

"You're such a bitch," he sneers at me, getting angry.

A tear falls down my cheek. "I'm sorry. Just go."

He shudders disgust at me, goes over to the table and grabs his phone, then pauses next to my front door. "You'll pay for this, Charlotte."

"Get out, Damon," I tell him.

He glares at me and leaves.

I lock the door, secure the dead bolt then collapse on the floor, crying.

What was I thinking?

I look at myself, naked except for a blanket, and shame overpowers me. When I stop crying, I grab my phone off the table and go into my bedroom. I put the phone on my charger on my nightstand and see that I have a message from Xander.

I crawl under the covers with my head spinning from all the alcohol.

"I did something really stupid," I message Xander.

I wish I could talk to you.

"Are you okay?" he responds.

"No. I'm not."

"Do you want to talk? I can give you my number if you want to talk?"

More torture. What have I been doing?

I have hit a low. *Is this what they call rock bottom?*

"No. I'm sorry, but I'm not going to be able to talk anymore."

"Okay. I'm here if you need me."

Here if you need me. Now that's just beyond cruel.

Xander

Present Day

WHEN THE EMAIL CAME ACROSS CHARLOTTE'S PHONE, I DIDN'T think twice about clicking on it. It said *HR INVESTIGATION UPDATE.*

I didn't want to wake her, but I didn't know if they would require any more information from her, so I opened it up.

The email said HR was looking into claims by Damon that Charlotte had been pursuing him and that he had proof their relationship was not over nine months ago. They were sharing the video with Charlotte so she could respond to the allegation and update her form appropriately.

I clicked on the video, and my gut flipped.

There was no audio. The date and time stamp showed two months ago. Charlotte was drinking something clear. She cringes every time she takes a sip then she and Damon are talking.

I don't like the fact that he is sitting on her couch next to her, but then he helps her stand up, and she strips. My pulse is beating in my neck when she's naked and crawls to him, before he pulls her up like a rag doll to straddle his lap.

The recording ends. I watch it several times, and it's clear to me Charlotte was drunk. Damon makes her drink several times, too.

I'm staring at Charlotte, who's asleep next to me, full of anger, when "NYSurgeon is waiting for you to make the next move" pops up on her phone.

The hair on my neck stands up. I click on the notification, and our last Words with Friends board pops up. It's the same game I stared at wondering why the game and conversation had stopped and if the player I had been talking to was okay.

I'd reached out several times over the last few months, asking if they were okay, but heard nothing.

Scrolling through our messages, I bang my head quietly against the headboard. The torture I must have put Charlotte through, always talking about Billie and my love for her. I cringe inside.

When I get back to the bottom of our messages, I read the date and time stamp of the last message.

Why is it bugging me?

Then, I realize it's the same date as the video. Charlotte's last message to me, "I did something really stupid," makes sense.

For hours, Charlotte sleeps on my arm. I think about how she was the only thing I looked forward to, all the months we played and talked on messenger. Guilt runs through me about how much pain I must have put her through, but she continued to be there for me, sacrificing her own feelings to make sure I was okay.

As much as I hate the visual of her being with Damon, I know that I caused her falling into his arms. And I decide the only thing I'm going to do is love and support her through this. She unselfishly did that for me without me even knowing it, and I'm going to be the man she needs me to be.

About twenty minutes pass, I figure she's had enough time to review the video, and I walk into the bedroom. Charlotte is sitting on the bed, looking shocked. I sit next to her and put my arm around her. Slowly, she looks over at me.

"I'm sorry."

"Shh. It's okay. You don't need to apologize." I kiss her on her forehead.

"This video. It's not what you think."

I pull her tighter to me. "Charlotte, it's okay."

She angrily pushes me away. "No, it's not okay."

"I didn't mean it like that."

"What do you mean, Xander? Let's get clear on this."

"I know you're upset, but I'm on your side. And this is my fault. You slept with him because of me and my messages. I drove you to it. I'm the one who should be apologizing."

She gapes at me and says nothing for a minute. "You're right, and you're wrong, Xander."

I tilt my head at her. "Fill me in, then."

"It's not okay he recorded me without my consent. It's not okay he stripped the audio from it and made it appear like we slept together. He cut off the part where I kicked him out. And it's not okay I lied to you all those months and kept talking to you. These were my choices, not yours."

I have no right to feel relieved she didn't sleep with him two months ago, but I do. I still don't have a clear picture of what happened that night. The only thing I can speak to is what's happened between us. "No, it isn't okay. And we will get to the bottom of this. But I'm glad you lied to me, or I wouldn't be standing here."

Charlotte's face scrunches. "What do you mean?"

I take a deep breath. "About a week after we started playing and talking. I had the pill bottles and a glass of water. I wrote a note. I was so frustrated because things were just too confusing, and I couldn't work or remember people or situations. I felt like it would never be okay again. I was ready to end it all, and your message popped up."

Shocked, she puts her hands on my face. "Xander, you'll kill me if you ever do anything like that."

I pull her on my lap. "I won't. I told you I was in a dark place. I'm out of it. But you saved me. If you hadn't lied to me, I wouldn't have talked to you."

"You wouldn't have?"

I shake my head. "No. But now that I know it was you, I know how much deeper I hurt you. I know whatever happened between you and Damon, my words caused it."

She closes her eyes and tears fall. "I only wanted you, and you didn't want me. He showed up, out of the blue. You had just told me about Billie, and I wasn't thinking clearly. I had isolated myself from everyone, and he was the first person I had any contact with in weeks. I shouldn't have let him in. I shouldn't have drunk with him. I shouldn't have done what he told me to do."

I pull her in close to me. "This isn't your fault."

"I made those choices."

"Shh. It's not your fault."

"What am I going to do about that video?"

"You're going to tell HR the truth and let them handle it. I'm going to call my attorney, and we're going to go after him."

She pulls her head back. "What do you mean?"

"It's illegal to record you in Illinois without your permission. I already looked it up. I'm going after the bastard, and we're going to make sure it doesn't go any further than those who have already seen it. He will pay."

She shakes her head. "Damon makes more than I do. He'll keep me in legal battles for years, just to screw with me."

"The attorneys will handle it. And you don't need to worry about the bill. I have more money than I know what to do with."

She squints at me. "I know you make good money as a surgeon, but Damon probably makes as much as you do, possibly more. He's been with my company longer."

"Can I tell you a secret?"

She nods.

I lean into her ear. "I'm filthy rich."

"I don't understand."

"I didn't, either. Trust me. It was confusing when Noah told me. But I invested with him when we were paramedics, and I own a lot of different companies. I reinvested almost everything, and I only work because I love it. So I have all these zeros behind my name, and nothing will make me happier than to use them to take Damon down."

She looks at me. "You're serious right now?"

"Yes. No one will mess with you."

"This doesn't make sense."

"What?"

"You saw the video, right?"

"Yes."

"But you aren't mad at me?"

"No."

"And you know I lied to you for months, but you aren't mad at me about that, either?"

"Nope."

"And you're going to hire a lawyer for me and take Damon down?"

"Yep."

"What's the catch?"

"There's no catch."

"What am I missing?"

Billie. We need to talk about Billie.

"There's one thing we still have to talk about."

Her face drops. "Billie."

I nod. "I want to discuss this, and then I don't want to talk about her ever again. You're the only person I love. The only person I want. I don't want you to question it going forward."

"Then why did you kiss her?"

"I did not kiss her. She was super drunk and threw herself on me, and I grabbed her by the waist because she was going to fall, and she kissed me. I tried to pull back, but she had me on lockdown."

Charlotte takes a deep breath. "She sure did have you on lockdown."

"I did not kiss her back." I'm looking into Charlotte's eyes, trying to find any doubt. If we are going to be together, she needs to believe me so we can move forward.

"Why was she in the coffee shop?"

"My bad luck. She showed up out of nowhere and pulled a chair up. No one invited her to sit."

Charlotte says nothing.

I cup her face in my hands. "Charlotte, I'm telling the truth."

She kisses me, and I feel all her belief and trust in me. I know this is our moment. "Are you ready to step off the roller coaster once and for all?"

"Together?"

"Yes, together."

She nods.

"No more going backward. Everything from now on is forward. You and I, together."

"You promise?" she whispers.

I smile and brush her lips with mine. "I promise."

"Good because I love you. Don't ever forget me again."

"I won't. I love you. Don't ever question it again."

28

EPILOGUE

Charlotte

A FEW WEEKS AFTER THE ACCIDENT, I WENT BACK TO WORK. During my time off, I disclosed to HR what happened the night Damon recorded the video. Xander didn't waste any time getting an attorney involved, and Damon recanted his claim I was harassing him, and we still were involved within a few weeks.

It didn't take long for HR to wrap up their investigation. He was fired, and Xander's attorneys continued to go after him.

We finally got the original version of the video, and Damon signed papers under oath he hadn't distributed the footage to anyone besides HR and this was the only copy.

It has been a few months since my accident, and Xander and I are in a comfortable routine. Since we are in most of the same surgeries, we leave for work and come home together almost every day. Even though we are together most of the day, Xander still finds moments to leave blueberry muffins, coffee, or other little gifts for me in my locker.

I'm about to close it when my phone beeps. The notification says, "NYSurgeon is waiting for you to make your next move."

I pause for a moment, thinking about all the memories I made with Xander playing this game. As tough as it was at times, there was a lot of laughter, too.

I open up the board and read my letters. Smiling, I write "heartbeat" and throw my phone in my locker.

Xander is already looking at the list for the day. He groans and turns to me. "Charlotte, you need to win rock, paper, scissors today. I can't do it again."

I laugh. "It was only a three-hour surgery. It could have been longer."

Xander puts his hand on my back and guides me out of the locker room. We are halfway down the hall when he says, "Hey, I have something to show you tonight. Don't make any plans."

"What's that?"

He grins at me. "I'm not telling you."

"You're going to make me wonder all day what it can be?"

He laughs. "Yep."

"You're evil."

He kisses me on the top of my head and opens the door to the operating room. Tabi smirks at me, and I smirk back as she puts our gloves on us.

Our day goes quickly, and after we shower and change, I pull out my phone and see a notification that Xander has just created a sixty-seven-point word. I write, "Nice job."

"Good to see you're back."

"I won't be going anywhere again."

"I'm going to give you some extra dessert tonight for writing that."

I laugh out loud, and Tabi looks at me. "What's so funny?"

"Nothing."

Xander has his bag, and he grabs mine. "Have a great night, Tabi."

"You, too." She smiles at him and smirks at me again.

We're walking down the hall, and Xander leans into me. "You're smoking hot."

I shake my head. He tells me that every day. "So, where are we going?"

"You'll see."

He guides me into the parking garage and opens the car passenger door for me.

"You're making me nervous," I tell him when he gets in the driver's side.

"Don't be nervous. It's nothing bad. So what do you rate the pus factor from patient number three today?"

I shrug. "It was kind of disappointing. I give it a five point three but was expecting more like an eight."

Xander laughs. "Yeah, I didn't see that coming, either. Total disappointment."

We fall into our banter that anyone else would think is gross and are soon pulling up to a building. Xander parks in the parking garage, and we get out. He leads me into the elevator and hits a code.

"Where are we?"

"You'll see." He winks at me, grinning.

When the elevator opens, we step into a massive empty shell, with floor-to-ceiling windows overlooking the entire city and the lake. It's spring, and there is no snow, but you can even see the ice skating rink.

Suddenly, Xander looks nervous. "I bought this for you."

I jerk back. "You bought this for me?"

"Yes."

"I don't understand."

He gets down on one knee, pulls out a stack of cards, and places them on the concrete. They are the cards he included when he sent me roses every week. Everyone says, *"Don't forget me"* and some form of *"I miss you."*

Blinking back tears, I stare at him.

Xander pulls out a massive diamond ring. "You never forgot me. And I didn't have all the pieces, but my heart was empty without you. I don't ever want to miss you again. I won't ever forget you again. I want you to have everything you never had...with me. So I bought you this penthouse so you can design it any way you want for our family. I want you to be my wife and forever mine. You're my sunshine, and I want to be yours. Will you marry me, Charlotte?"

As I stare into his eyes, our journey together races through my mind. There's been so much pain, but all I can see is love.

"Yes," I whisper to him as tears fall from both our eyes. "Yes, I'll marry you."

He slides the ring on my finger and pulls me into him, kissing me with so much love, I wonder how I ever existed without him.

"I love you," I whisper to him.

"Thank you for loving me through everything." He kisses me again, and I pull back and look at the ring.

"It's beautiful." I tell him.

Xander stands up, pulling me into him.

I lace my hands around his head.

He smiles. "You did that the first time we kissed."

I nod.

"I've been trying to figure that out. We were on the dance floor."

"Yes."

He traces my lips with his finger. "Do you like the penthouse? If you don't like it, we can get something else."

I laugh. "It's amazing."

"Yeah?"

"Yeah. Thank you."

He shows me around, and we stand in front of the windows. He is behind me, his arms around my waist. After he kisses the top of my head, he says, "Okay, time to go."

I glance up at him. "Why?"

"We have a game to play tonight."

"Medical Term Scrabble?"

He laughs. "Nope."

I look at him in question.

A cocky grin comes on his face. "Dirty Doctor."

I laugh. "Dirty Doctor?"

He nods and with a sly look says, "Yes. And my patient has requested I be extra filthy."

Ready to read Chase and Vivian's story?

Click here to read My Friend the Billionaire!

MY FRIEND THE BILLIONAIRE BLURB
IT'S COMPLICATED - BOOK THREE

————

I'M KEEPING CHASE MONROE IN THE FRIEND ZONE.

He's doing everything possible to move me out of it.

He's the living embodiment of the billionaire playboy—richer than God, sexy as sin, and charming as hell.

With a full calendar of friends-with-benefits.

His strict no-relationships policy means I'd be another notch on his bedpost.

Not happening.

But our friendship is hard to keep.

Every innocent touch leads to more cravings we can't deny.

He claims he just has to show me how good we can be together.

I almost cave until I realize what's happening.

So I force him to make a choice.

But Chase's "harmless" past runs deeper than I could ever imagine.

So deep it's deadly.

Click here to continue reading My Friend the Billionaire!

MY FRIEND THE BILLIONAIRE - PROLOGUE & PART OF CHAPTER ONE

BOOK THREE OF IT'S COMPLICATED

Chase Monroe

Eight years ago

THE CATALYST OF OUR CHOICES IS OFTEN PEOPLE OR SITUATIONS WE wish we could forget. These become moments in life that shape and guide our decisions going forward. Good or bad, the new beliefs we hold because of the past allow us to stay stuck or move forward. And if we're stuck, we lie to ourselves that we're in control of our lives because the rules we now follow are on our side.

But what happens when we create walls so thick no one can get through? When our new truths become toxic, but we don't realize it? And the protection we create for our hearts is just a mirage?

For three years, I save my money, work doubles, and invest in companies Noah insists I need to. I'm on a tight budget, but I'm putting money aside in a different account—a bucket meant for her.

Finally, I've saved enough. I visit the jeweler and help design a ring. I choose a flawless one-carat, princess-cut diamond. That's what she is to me—my princess.

Several weeks later, the ring is finished, and I return to the jeweler's.

"She must be a special woman," he says.

"She is the most special woman."

The jeweler chuckles. "Well, she will be crazy not to love this." He opens the box that is on the glass counter and shows me the finished ring.

I grab the ring out of the box. "It's perfect."

"I wish you many happy years," the jeweler says.

"Thank you. I have no doubt we will have them." I pay the remaining balance and head back to my house. Jennifer is working today. We live together, and I need to hide the ring until Saturday. That's when I will propose, and I have everything all planned out.

As I'm approaching my house, I see Matt and Jennifer's cars in the driveway. *Why is Matt here at two in the afternoon? Why is Jennifer not at work?*

Matt's been my friend since grade school. I've had two friends who have been through everything with me—Matt and Jamison. I trust them with my life and would die for them.

I pull into the driveway behind Matt's car. Putting the ring box in my coat pocket, I go to open the door, but it's locked. *That's strange.*

Fishing my keys out of my pocket, I quickly unlock the door and expect to see Jennifer and Matt in the living area or the kitchen that opens up to that room, but they aren't there.

Where are they? The only other room in our house is the bedroom or bathroom. I'm about to call out their names, but something in my gut tells me not to.

Maybe they're in the backyard? It's cold out, but anything is possible.

I'm heading toward the back door when I hear it.

"Oh God." Jennifer's voice comes through the door.

"Yeah, baby," Matt's voice follows.

The hair on my neck stands up, and, for a brief moment, I stare at the door to the bedroom, paralyzed. *Surely I heard that wrong?*

"Faster," Jennifer calls out.

Anger fills every cell of my body as I open the door and see Matt, naked on top of Jennifer. Her legs are around him, and she's digging her nails into his back and moaning.

I don't say anything. As quickly as I can move, I'm ripping Matt off her.

"Chase!" Jennifer cries out.

Surprise fills Matt's face before I land several punches on him.

"Chase, stop!" Jennifer screams as I continue to pummel him.

He recovers and defends himself by punching me back and lands one on my cheek.

I step back. "Get out of my house."

Jennifer stands up, naked, and tries to find her clothes. "Chase—"

"Don't." I cut her off. "You both have ten seconds to get out of my house."

"I live here. You can't just kick me out. Let's talk about this," Jennifer pleads with me.

I sneer. "There is nothing for us to talk about. Get out."

"Chase—" Matt tries as he grabs his clothes off the floor.

"Don't you ever talk to me again. Get out."

Sadness passes through his eyes, but he walks past me with his clothes in his hands.

"Please, let's talk," she pleads.

I point to the door. "We are done. Out."

Sadly, she throws on her clothes. "This is your fault. If you hadn't been working so much, I wouldn't have felt so lonely."

Enraged, I yell, "Working so much? I was working to pay for a ring. One that I picked up today."

Shock registers on her face then she steps closer to me and puts her hand on my arm. "We can get past this."

I pull my arm free. "It's over. Get out."

"Let's try. We can't throw away five years."

I snarl, "You threw it away when you slept with my best friend. Now get out."

"We can still get married," she says quickly.

I shake my head in disgust then walk out to the main room. "Both of you better be gone by the time I get back." I pass Matt, whose face is bloody and swelling, and I'm tempted to beat him again, but I'm afraid I'll kill him.

I get into my car and drive off. As the shock and anger wane, grief replaces them. About a mile away, I pull over and park at the back of the grocery store lot. Tears flow out of my eyes so fast, I sob.

At this moment, the wall forms. I create a lie. My new truth seems honest. I tell myself it's to protect my heart.

Unfortunately, my new reality is an invisible toxic web, but I can't see the poison that I weave.

CHAPTER ONE

Vivian

Present Day

QUICKSAND SUCKS YOU IN, TRYING TO SUBMERGE YOU ENTIRELY SO you can't breathe or move away from it. Its victims are powerless. They struggle to free themselves, but that only immerses them deeper into the deadly grasp.

Chase Monroe is my quicksand. I need to figure out how to pull myself out of his hold.

Several times I escaped him. Or so I thought. He always comes back, piercing me deeper.

"Chase and Jamison are in town this weekend. Come out to Club D with us Friday night, so I'm not by myself," the text from Piper says.

My heart is a mix of flutters and dread. I should not see Chase anymore. We cannot be, and every time I am near him, I only want him more.

"You'll have Noah," I text Piper, stalling while I debate in my head if I should go or not.

Rationally, I know I shouldn't.

Emotionally, I'm dying to see him again.

As I'm conversing with myself in my head, I get another message. This time, it's not from Piper.

"Am I going to see you this weekend?" The text from Chase pops up on the screen, and butterflies erupt in my stomach.

He wants to see me.

Of course, he does. He wants you to be another one of his girls.

Tell him no.

Against my better judgment, I play dumb. "Are you in Chicago?"

"Yep. You didn't hear?"

"Sorry. I have a life besides keeping up on your schedule."

"Fair enough. Friday night. Club D. I think we should dance."

"How do I know you won't step on my toes all night."

"Come out, and you'll find out."

I'm grappling with myself about whether to go or not when I get another text from him.

"I miss you. Please tell me you'll come."

And those words make me once again lose the battle.

"Okay. I'll see you on Friday."

…

Click here to continue reading My Friend the Billionaire!

ALL IN BOXSET

Three page-turning, interconnected stand-alone romance novels with HEA's!! Get ready to fall in love with the characters. Billionaires. Professional athletes. New York City. Twist, turns, and danger lurking everywhere. The only option for these couples is to go ALL IN...with a little help from their friends. EXTRA STEAM INCLUDED!

Grab it now! READ FREE IN KINDLE UNLIMITED!

CAN I ASK YOU A HUGE FAVOR?

Would you be willing to leave me a review?

I would be forever grateful as one positive review on Amazon is like buying the book a hundred times! Reader support is the lifeblood for Indie authors and provides us the feedback we need to give readers what they want in future stories!

Your positive review means the world to me! So thank you from the bottom of my heart!

CLICK TO REVIEW

MORE BY MAGGIE COLE

It's Complicated Series (Series Two - Chicago Billionaires)

My Boss the Billionaire - Book One

Forgotten by the Billionaire - Book Two

My Friend the Billionaire - Book Three

Forbidden Billionaire - Book Four

The Groomsman Billionaire - Book Five

Secret Mafia Billionaire - Book Six

Mafia Wars New York - A Dark Mafia Series (Series Six)

Toxic (Dante's Story) - Book One

Immoral (Gianni's Story) - Book Two

Crazed (Massimo's Story) - Book Three

Carnal (Tristano's Story) - Book Four

Flawed (Luca's Story) - Book Five

Mafia Wars - A Dark Mafia Series (Series Five)

Ruthless Stranger (Maksim's Story) - Book One

Broken Fighter (Boris's Story) - Book Two

Cruel Enforcer (Sergey's Story) - Book Three

Vicious Protector (Adrian's Story) - Book Four

Savage Tracker (Obrecht's Story) - Book Five

Unchosen Ruler (Liam's Story) - Book Six

Perfect Sinner (Nolan's Story) - Book Seven

Brutal Defender (Killian's Story) - Book Eight

Deviant Hacker (Declan's Story) - Book Nine

Relentless Hunter (Finn's Story) - Book Ten

Behind Closed Doors (Series Four - Former Military Now International Rescue Alpha Studs)

Depths of Destruction - Book One

Marks of Rebellion - Book Two

Haze of Obedience - Book Three

Cavern of Silence - Book Four

Stains of Desire - Book Five

Risks of Temptation - Book Six

Together We Stand Series (Series Three - Family Saga)

Kiss of Redemption- Book One

Sins of Justice - Book Two

Acts of Manipulation - Book Three

Web of Betrayal - Book Four

Masks of Devotion - Book Five

Roots of Vengeance - Book Six

All In Series (Series One - New York Billionaires)

The Rule - Book One

The Secret - Book Two

The Crime - Book Three

The Lie - Book Four

The Trap - Book Five

The Gamble - Book Six

Stand Alone Christmas Novella

Judge Me Not

ABOUT THE AUTHOR

Amazon Bestselling Author

Maggie Cole is committed to bringing her readers alphalicious book boyfriends. She's an international bestselling author and has been called the "literary master of steamy romance." Her books are full of raw emotion, suspense, and will always keep you wanting more. She is a masterful storyteller of contemporary romance and loves writing about broken people who rise above the ashes.

Maggie lives in Florida with her son. She loves sunshine, anything to do with water, and everything naughty.

Her current series were written in the order below:

- All In

- It's Complicated (Together We Stand (Brooks Family Saga - read in order)
- Behind Closed Doors (Read in order)
- Mafia Wars
- Mafia Wars New York

Maggie Cole's Newsletter
Sign up here!

Hang Out with Maggie in Her Reader Group
Maggie Cole's Romance Addicts

Follow for Giveaways
Facebook Maggie Cole

Instagram
@maggiecoleauthor

Complete Works on Amazon
Follow Maggie's Amazon Author Page

Book Trailers
Follow Maggie on YouTube

Are you a Blogger and want to join my ARC team?
Signup now!

Feedback or suggestions?
Email: authormaggiecole@gmail.com

Made in the USA
Coppell, TX
12 January 2023

10983621R00173